One of the most innovative and hu̱......... ..... 1 have ever read.
A must read. —Michael A. Burstein, John W. Campbell Award winner

I love time travel stories. One of my first novels involved time travel (spoiler alert: it's a secret plot twist).

Time travel stories tend to be either wild adventures (like *Back to the Future*) or intellectual "what-if" scenarios (like *The Man Who Folded Himself*). This one falls into the second group, where part of the fun is working out the paradoxes and problems that time travel can create and seeing how the main character deals with them. As *Time On My Hands* progressed, however, a new previously unseen plot emerged which turned this from a simple intellectual exercise into a different kind of mystery with a satisfying conclusion.

Fast paced, with interesting characters, humor, and of course, some movie references (this is Daniel Kimmel, after all). —Michael A. Ventrella, author of *Bloodsuckers* and the *Arch Enemies* series

In *Time On My Hands*, Dan Kimmel has crafted a sweet shaggy-dog tale of philosophy and paradox in which it's never too late for true love or redemption, even if you're a time traveler. —LJ Cohen, author of the Halcyone Space series

Also by Daniel M. Kimmel:

Shh! It's a Secret: a novel about Aliens, Hollywood, and the Bartender's Guide

2014 Compton Crook Award Finalist

[A] freewheeling, laugh-out-loud satire of the movie industry. —*Publishers Weekly*

This first novel by Kimmel… throws caution to the winds as it spins a whimsical, amiable satire on alien first encounters, the movie industry, and American society. —*Library Journal*

[Kimmel's first novel is] a true joy… let's hope there are more to come. —Don Sakers, *Analog Science Fiction and Fact*

This is the book we've been waiting for from Dan Kimmel—funny, knowing, fast paced, full of humor, and told with a big heart. An absolute joy. —Robert J. Sawyer, multiple Hugo Award winner

Dan Kimmel's first novel is a funny and delightful tour de force that will appeal to movie fans as well as science-fiction readers. —Michael A. Burstein, John W. Campbell Award winner

Dan Kimmel's first novel is as witty, smart, and funny as his non-fiction books. In large part, this stems from Kimmel's unrestrained sense of fun, as he takes aim at Tinseltown and scores one direct hit after another. Kimmel's love of science fiction and expertise in the genre also comes to the fore… but above all else this is a book about friendship and family…. Odd-couple antics are inevitable, but Kimmel avoids the obvious pitfalls and lays his plot more carefully than is typical for the first contact / comedy genre. The culture clashes take on a more mature cast…. Kimmel has a natural comic talent that comes through at every turn: Plotting, prose style, characters, and even the chapter names, which are borrowed from the titles of classic films…. Kimmel even comes up with a new twist on the old joke about foods that taste like chicken—to say more would be to spoil a major development…. you'll be surprised at how many cultural strands Kimmel has woven together. The laughs we can almost take for granted: Kimmel is a funny guy. What's most satisfying about this novel is that it's not just a bunch of gags strung together… rather, it's a novel first and foremost, and the way it taps into a wellspring of intelligent, family-friendly humor gives it that much more loft and speed. —Kilian Melloy, *EDGE on the Net*

A brisk fun read despite it almost being too good natured for its own good!… *Shh! It's a Secret* is filled with the sort of small details that makes a piece of fiction feel very real (except for the blue-skinned aliens of course). It is a brisk and light read but will keep you pressing that "Next Page" button on your Kindle just to see what happens next. —James O'Ehley, *SciFi Movie Page*

Kimmel's debut novel is brilliant satire of the film industry, which also happens to be a hilarious, heartwarming science fiction story about unexpected friendship…. Kimmel's voice is very distinct with a droll sense of humor…. Kimmel's yarn is a fast-paced, enjoyable read that bounces between several exciting locations: Los Angeles, New York City, and the Catskills. There's also amazing suspense in the build-up to the premiere of Abe's film. What's most surprising though, is the touching friendship that slowly develops between Abe and Jake. —Evan Crean, *StarPulse.com*

Exceptionally funny… pretty damned spectacular… this is the funniest book of the year and one of the best debut SF novels in ages! —Chris Garcia, *The Drink Tank*

Kimmel is no stranger to the movie industry or science fiction, and it shows in nearly every page of the novel…. The story casts a light-hearted, satirical eye on the foibles of Hollywood, showing a keen understanding of the industry. The humor is slow cooked rather than rapid-fire, mature rather than juvenile…. *Shh! It's a Secret* is a wacky first contact story that could only happen in Hollywood. It is the sort of novel that will appeal to a broad readership, especially those who enjoy a witty Hollywood yarn or a humorous science fiction tale. *Shh!* stands as the funniest mix of film making and first contact since William Tenn gave the Venusians the Hollywood treatment in *Venus and the Seven Sexes*. —David Kilman, *Amazing Stories*

Jar Jar Binks Must Die…
and Other Observations about Science Fiction Movies

2012 Hugo Award finalist for Best Related Work

A spirited explanation of the role of science fiction films in our culture. Any serious fan of the cinema must read this book. —Michael A. Burstein, John W. Campbell Award winner

Kimmel displays expertise on the subject along with a lively sense of humor—scarcely a page is turned that doesn't yield a few good laughs…. Readers who already take science fiction seriously will enjoy the book's panoptic breadth and it's frank jubilation in its subject matter…. [Kimmel] makes it his business to guide his readers to science fiction films that are worthy of our attention as social commentary, whiz-bang spectacle, or works of entertainment that carry an extra edge…. the best advice to take with you on your foray into *Jar Jar Binks Must Die* is this: keep your Netflix wish list at the ready. You're going to revisit movies you hadn't thought about in years and be irresistibly tantalized by films you've never seen, and maybe never even heard of. —Kilian Melloy, *Edge Boston*

[Kimmel's] writing is intelligent and entertaining…. his knowledge of SF movies is encyclopedic…. This is the guy you want sitting next to you when Channel 45 has a weekend "sci-fi" movie marathon…. For anyone who likes SF movies, this volume is worth the price of admission. —Don Sakers, *Analog Science Fiction and Fact*

...the leading film voice in fandom today... Dan's look at all the SF Films of the previous century-plus is powerful and serious and smart and even sassy at points.... His look at *Metropolis* and *Things to Come* are both brilliant and much deeper and broader than mine in these pages.... I thought it was the best written look at *Destination Moon* I've ever read.... I could spend a day heaping praise on the essay "Our Batman".... So many great pieces in here that I should just say this is the best book of essays about film of any nature that I've read in ages.... the best pieces of writing on SF Film you'll ever see! —Chris Garcia, *The Drink Tank*

...one is left wanting more, which is a testament to Kimmel's writing abilities.... Even when you find yourself not agreeing with Kimmel—his take on *E.T.* is just plain wrong damn it!—the book remains worthwhile and thought-provoking.... *Jar Jar Binks Must Die* is worth a purchase. —*Sci-Fi Movie Page*

Kimmel's a terrific guide to classic though underappreciated works such as *Things to Come*, and is especially sharp on 1950s sf movies, David Cronenberg, and the art (or lack of same) of movie remakes.... his brief essays are addictively readable and yes, a lot more fun than watching *Revenge of the Sith*. —Elizabeth Hand, *The Magazine of Fantasy & Science Fiction*

[Kimmel's] essays are both informed and informative, erudite, often humorous, filled with insider-knowledge... [the book] is eminently accessible—and has a few good points to make.... *Jar Jar Binks Must Die* has now become the sourcebook that I will use to underpin my [film] arguments, as Daniel has said everything I've been saying about film, although much more so and in a far more entertaining and convincing manner.... This is an encyclopedic mind at work, one that went looking for the redeeming qualities in just about any of Hollywood's SF efforts and managed to find something in most of them.... *Jar Jar Binks Must Die* is a well put together book; Fantastic Books has created a handy tome that is easy to read and well-organized. —Steve Davidson, *Amazing Stories*

Time On My Hands:

My Misadventures in Time Travel

by Daniel M. Kimmel

In-house editor: Ian Randal Strock

Fantastic Books
1380 East 17 Street, Suite 2233
Brooklyn, New York 11230
www.FantasticBooks.biz

First Edition ISBN 10: 1-5154-0052-2
First Edition ISBN 13: 978-1-5154-0052-3

First Edition

Dedicated to the memory of my great-aunt
Bina Itzkowitz
Who encouraged me to read and
gave me the freedom to write

Table of Contents

"One always has time enough, if one will apply it well."
—Johann Wolfgang von Goethe

"Its provenance?"

"Yes. See, it appears that I may have invented it sometime in the future. I haven't found out yet. Naturally, I have no memory of this because I haven't done it yet."

If I slip the phone into my pocket I can be out the door in about ten seconds, thought Miller. However, he had been sent out to get a story, and he had to at least try. It was that sense of professionalism that had served him well in the past. You do what you're supposed to do. "Okay, Professor Price, I have to admit I'm thoroughly confused."

The academic leaned back and laughed. It wasn't the laugh of a crazy man. It was the laugh of a man who got the joke. "Confused, Mr. Miller? You have no idea. If you find it confusing, how do you think I felt when I walked into my office one morning and discovered that I was already here?"

PAIR OF DOCS

I was an associate professor in the '90s, fully expecting to get tenure but not quite there yet. I was still required to teach a certain number of introductory courses that the fully tenured faculty could, with a few deft steps, manage to avoid. One such class was physics for those taking up space at the university on athletic scholarships. These were the so-called "gut" courses. Anyone who was actually paying attention in class could easily pass them. Yet, you'd be surprised at the number of students who could screw up an easy A or B, even when it was being handed to them on a platter. You've heard of "Rocks for Jocks," the gimme course that departments of geology often offer? The physics department offering was called—among the faculty, anyway—"Quarks for Dorks." Lucky me, I got to teach it.

I got to campus not long before my 11 A.M. class would be held. There wasn't much to do in the way of preparation, and it's not like someone there on a basketball scholarship wanted to meet with me to talk about new research in sub-atomic particles. When I got to my office, I was surprised to see the door was ajar. I could be forgetful, but as I was only in my late twenties, it was a bit early to start cultivating that "absent-minded professor" persona. When I opened the door, I was stunned to discover a much older man sitting at my desk as if he owned the place.

"It's about time you got here," he growled, as if I was the one who was the transgressor, rather than he.

"Who the hell are you, and what are you doing in my office?" I demanded, fairly certain I had a better than even chance against a man in his late fifties, even if I hadn't actually wrestled with anyone since tenth grade gym class. Rather than reel back at my display of machismo, the old man sighed and waved his hand, bidding me entrance into my own office.

"Don't worry. I'm not trying to threaten you. Quite the contrary. Could you please come in and close the door?" With that, he got up and walked toward a stool at the work station at the rear of my office. It was clear he was making a point of ceding my desk to me. I stepped in and closed the door, but did not yet take his place. It seemed prudent to maintain the

"Embarrassing? How is it… Now stop that!" He had continued to echo my words.

"I'm sorry, but I need to convince you that this is real and you need to take the machine."

I closed my mouth and waved him on. Obviously he had an agenda to go through, and the quicker he did it, the quicker this bizarre incident could be over and I could see if my health insurance through the university covered psychiatric treatment. "I know you're trying to figure out some explanation proving that this isn't real," he continued. "It is. And all I can really tell you is that the machine is now yours to experiment with, and that you will conduct a number of experiments that will change our understanding of time, as well as transform my… er, your… well, I guess it would be *our* lives. Unfortunately grammar hasn't quite caught up with science yet."

"Okay, but why do I have to do it? You invented the thing. Why don't you conduct these experiments?" I thought I had him now. This ought to be good.

Instead, he slumped back in his seat. "This is the way it has to be. See, I didn't invent the machine either. I think it was invented by us further down the time line, but the only way I know I initially discovered it was by receiving it today, by being where you are right now. My theory is that, for reasons you'll come to understand someday, our future self needed for you to conduct these experiments as a young man and that somehow that research is what ultimately allowed him to invent the device and for you to improve upon it."

That bottle of single malt was beginning to look a lot more necessary. "So if I got it from you and you got it from me as I get older, where did it come in the first place?"

"*That's* one of the things I have yet to figure out and I've had nearly thirty years to do it. Solving that mystery is one of the things that has been keeping me going, and why I had to get the time machine back to you." We both sat there quietly for a moment, only one of us knowing what would happen next. Once again he anticipated my next move. "When you take out the Glenfiddich, pour some for me as well."

Now picture this: there are two of me sitting in my cramped office, thirty years apart in age, sharing a twelve-year-old scotch. It was certainly not how I had planned to spend my day, especially as it was not yet noon. "To science," I said, at a loss for a more appropriate toast.

"To Time," he responded, lifting his glass.

"Okay, now what? Are you going to tell me the experiments I have to conduct? Since you already conducted them, are they even necessary? Can't you just tell me what you found?"

"Ah, now we get to the nature of time. Do you remember how Mark Twain defined it? The time of your life, he said, was just one damned thing after another. He wasn't wrong, but it turns out to be a bit more complicated than that. Remember the science fiction stories about time travel we've read? What happened in them?"

I sipped the amber liquid, which was starting to taste like I needed more. There was a slight, not unpleasant burn which was most welcome at the moment, because it told me I was awake and not dreaming all this. "Well, the protagonist went into the past or the future and had various adventures."

"Let's stick with the past for the moment. Is it possible to go back in time and change the past? Einstein would have said no, but yet here I am. In fact, there are experiments that will occur in the next decade or so that show some sub-atomic particles actually travel backward in time. But in those stories we read in our youth, what happens when someone tries to change the past?"

I had to think about it for a moment. I had read a great deal of science fiction when I was young, but hadn't read much fiction of any sort in the last several years, as my focus was on getting tenure. When they say "Publish or perish" they don't mean writing *Star Trek* reviews. I did seem to remember a couple of stories, though, that had completely opposite takes on the matter of time travel. "It all depends on the story. Ray Bradbury's 'A Sound of Thunder' has a man step on a butterfly in prehistoric times and when he comes back to the present, it was completely transformed. Alfred Bester's 'The Men Who Murdered Mohammad' had people making vast changes in history that didn't affect anyone but themselves."

The older me smiled. "They were both wrong. If you want to understand time, you'd be better off reading Twain's *Life on the Mississippi*. Time is like a river. If I toss a pebble into the river, it is changed, but nothing really important has changed at all. If I build a dam across it, the river is severely changed. For reasons I'm still trying to understand, the laws of Time will allow you to toss pebbles, but not build dams."

It took me a moment to grasp what he was saying, but then I got it. "So one can make small changes but not big ones."

He looked a little pained. Then he took my bottle of scotch and poured us both another round. "You're going to need this," he said replacing the cap. "What you said is correct, but it doesn't answer the larger question."

There was a knock at the door. "I'm busy," we both shouted simultaneously, and we could hear whomever it was scurry away. Perhaps it was the scotch on an empty stomach, but I was now engaged with the scientific problem, even if part of me still didn't believe it was possible. "Okay, I'll bite. What's the larger question?"

"What's a small change and what's a big change?" And with that, he gulped down the rest of his glass and stood up. "And that's the subject matter for the experiments you're about to conduct."

"I would think it would be obvious. It's the difference between the pebble and the dam."

He gave me a rueful smile. "I just handed you a time machine. Isn't that going to be one of the biggest changes in history? And yet I had no problem at all doing that. However if I had tried to let your T.A. in a moment ago—he'll be back in a few minutes asking for the grading sheet —I wouldn't have been able to do it."

"How do you know? Oh, because you've already done the experiments…"

"You'll see for yourself. You'll *have* to see for yourself. I have tried to quantify what changes Time permits, but haven't been able to come up with a solid rule. Whether it's by whim or, as some would have it, a higher authority, I don't know. We do have free will in the sense that you'll freely make the choices that I've already made, and if I tried to tell you what they were, something would prevent me from doing so. Giving you the machine is okay, but telling you that you'll meet…" His voice suddenly gave out and all he could do was gasp. He reached for his glass, but it was empty. I went to pour him some more, but he put up his hands.

"I'm fine. It was just a small demonstration of how you can't break the laws of Time… whatever they might be. You'll see that for yourself. And now," he said, "I have to go." He headed to the door.

"But how? I have the time machine. And where are you going to? Back to your own time?"

"I can't say… literally," he said with a rueful smile. Then he came over and embraced me. When he stood back, he looked at me. "I really was a dashing figure in my youth. It was a pleasure getting a taste of it from the beginning. From *before* the beginning. Goodbye, Willy. I envy you the journey I took so long ago." And before I could stop him, he was out the door, which he closed behind him. I rushed out into the hallway after him, but he was gone. Classes had just broken, and the hallway was filled with students heading toward lunch.

"Professor Price?" I turned to see my T.A. heading towards me. "I figured you were in class. I just needed…"

"The grading sheet, I know. Come, let me get it for you." I didn't bother to acknowledge the look of astonishment on his face as I headed back into my office.

TIME FRAME

Professor Price sat back in his seat with a sigh. That was a tough story to share, and the effort had taken its toll. Miller was impressed with the effort, if not the details. Clearly, this addled academic *believed* the yarn he had just recounted, even if it was utterly preposterous. For one thing, it made the alleged time machine sound like a *deus ex machina*, something that had been introduced by the gods and could not otherwise be explained. Clearly, there was no story here. At most, his lead would be that a delusional physics professor was not only still on the payroll at his alma mater, but was allowed to teach classes, making him a danger to himself and to others. Price seemed harmless and genial enough, but how could anyone trust someone so disconnected from reality?

Price's next words took the reporter by surprise. "I don't expect you to believe me, young man, at least not yet."

The reporter took him at his word. "So are you going to offer me some proof? Perhaps take me on a trip to see the dinosaurs?"

The academic rolled his eyes. "Always the dinosaurs. No, Mr. Miller, I'm not going to take you to 'Jurassic Park'. All I ask is that you hear me out. If when I'm done you think I'm just an old fool, you can walk away without obligation. I'm not crazy, but I realize the burden of proof is on me to convince you of that fact. All I ask is that you give me the chance." He fixed his gaze on Miller with such intensity and sincerity that the reporter was slightly taken aback. This was a man who clearly understood how deranged he sounded. All he was asking was for a chance to demonstrate that he was for real. It wasn't like Miller had anywhere else to go at the moment. He was on assignment. If, as expected, the story came to naught, the onus was on the idiot editor who had assigned him to this fool's errand in the first place.

"Okay, Professor Price. Let's assume for the moment that I believe you. Now what? Are you prepared to give this gift to the world? According to your own story, this seems to be something from the future, not our own time. Why go public now?"

Professor Price offered the reporter a genial smile. He understood he had won a round. The cynical young reporter didn't really believe him, but he was willing to hear him out and suspend his disbelief in the meantime. Given the fantastic nature of the story, could he really expect any other response? Indeed, it was the best response he could have gotten at this point. He would take his victories where he could get them and move on.

"Thank you, Mr. Miller. I understand that you are skeptical, but I appreciate your open mindedness more than I can say. Let me ask for one other small concession, if I may."

The young man looked at the professor. Why was he listening to this crackpot at all? Maybe it was just the residual good feelings he had being back on the campus where he had finally blossomed into adulthood. There was no question he had many positive associations with the school, from his time on the campus newspaper to his two-year relationship with the features editor of that newspaper. He couldn't help it. He had never quite severed his connections to his college days. If Price had been teaching at any other school in the city, he would have already been gone. Here, though, there was an emotional bond that was, admittedly, not wholly rational, and though the professor couldn't possibly know that, it certainly was something that he had inadvertently been able to tap into to his advantage.

"Concession?" he asked quizzically.

"Call me Willy," said the professor. "And, if I may, I'd like to address you as Max. I have much more to relate, and 'Professor Price' and 'Mr. Miller' is not only cumbersome, but time consuming."

The professor was an odd bird indeed, thought the reporter. Again, the man's simplicity and sincerity cut through the cynicism. What harm could it do? "Okay… Willy."

"Wonderful… Max."

"So, you have a time machine. What do you do with it? Change history? Have sex with Cleopatra and Helen of Troy? Witness Moses on Sinai, or Jesus on the cross?"

Price offered the reporter a smile. "Those are good questions, and I'll answer them in a moment, but you're missing the question you ought to be asking first."

This rankled the reporter. As with many people relatively new on the job, he harbored the secret fear that he would be exposed as not really up to the requirements of his profession. "What am I missing?" Miller tried to keep his tone even, but he couldn't help a bit of huffiness.

"Please, Max, I didn't mean to offend you. I'm simply suggesting that the first thing you might ask is to see the time machine itself. And then I would tell you why you can't."

Okay, thought Miller, *in for a penny, in for a pound.* "So, let me see your time machine. Oh, I can't. Why not?"

"The machine that my future self brought to me is safely locked away. It's something that I'll need to pass on to my past self some day, and is a special version of the device. Go ahead. Ask me, 'Why?'"

Now the reporter was getting annoyed. It was one thing to play along with an addled interview subject in hopes of eventually getting to a story. It was quite another thing to be patronized. "Willy? Why don't you let *me* ask the questions, okay?"

"I'm sorry. I guess I'm too used to lecturing college students. You're right, of course. You're the reporter. I have a story to tell, but you need to elicit it in your own fashion. Please go ahead."

Miller wasn't sure why he didn't just leave, but instead he looked at Price and said, "Okay, why can't I see your time machine?"

"You can see *my* time machine. What would be the purpose of bringing you here if I couldn't show you that?"

The reporter felt like he had fallen down the rabbit hole. "Can we please stop playing games? I can see the time machine but I can't see the time machine but I can. I don't even know what I'm saying. Can you just cut to the chase?"

"I understand this is very confusing. I've been living with this for many years and it's all new to you. So let's start with the device. My future self brought me a working time machine. Once I had determined it was real...," he held up his hands to cut off the reporter's response, "I'll get to that in a minute. Once I had determined it was real, my next step was to do a bit of reverse engineering to see how it was put together and determine how I could create a duplicate device. What I found was profoundly interesting."

Miller was ready to give up at this point. "And what you found was...?"

"Every single part of the time machine—every circuit, computer chip, wire, and so on—was made of material that was readily available to me at the time. It was not a 'future' device. It was something that could be built in my present. Indeed, over time I would work out several ways to improve it as our technology advanced and I came to understand temporal mechanics, but I realized that it was important to preserve the original device to give to myself in the future... or in the past, so to speak. So as I built first a duplicate version and then, over the years, increasingly advanced models, I made sure that the original device was stored somewhere where it would be safe. Someday I will take that artifact into the past and give it to my younger self. Meanwhile, as I continued to learn about the nature of time travel, I tweaked the device that I actually used. Now I understood why my future self could leave what I came to think of as the 'original' with me and yet return to his own time without it."

Miller's head hurt. The story was getting more and more preposterous, and yet it did have a certain internal logic to it. He had no choice but to ask the obvious next question.

"Okay. You had a time machine. You understood how it worked and could not only replicate the technology, but eventually improve upon it. What did you do then?"

"I could ask you what *you* would have done then, but we'll come to that in good time. What *I* did was try to prevent myself from having a cup of coffee."

HOT WATER

So I had a time machine, or at least that's what I had been told. The first order of business was to see if it actually worked. If it did, I would have plenty of time—literally—to go into the past and change things for the better or go into the future to see what was in store. I decided that I would keep my first jaunt simple. I would just go for a few hours into the past and see if I could catch my future self arriving at my office.

The original device was about the size of a billfold, but the controls were easy enough to figure out. I could set the time and the date and then press a button to go there. Later, I would learn that there were various internal controls that compensated for things like the Earth's rotation and orbit. This was fortunate, because if there hadn't been, going even a few hours into the past while remaining in the same place would have put me in space. I found I could manipulate those controls as well, so I could travel in space and time, although leaving the planet was not something I contemplated doing. Indeed, to this day I have not tried to leave Earth, for all the obvious reasons, starting with the fact that I had no way of knowing if I'd end up somewhere on a planet with a breathable atmosphere or, indeed, with any atmosphere at all.

Instead, I decided that I should begin with the simplest possible experiment. I went back in time three hours, to 9 A.M., two hours before I had actually arrived at my office. The transition was imperceptible. I set the time and the date, pressed the button, and when I looked, up the clock had moved back three hours. Nothing else had changed. Well, that's not quite true. My office was exactly the same, but when I opened my bottom drawer, there was the bottle of water I would gulp down in a couple of hours, and the bottle of scotch hadn't been touched. If this was a hoax concocted by my friends, such things would have been easy to fix, but then "future me" popped into the office at 9:30. One moment I was alone, and the next moment I was not.

He looked at me for a moment with a bit of confusion, as if surprised I was there. Then he said, "Right, I forgot the first thing I did was go back earlier that morning. Okay. You've seen the machine works. Now go away. You're going to be here in an hour or so, and we really don't need three of us here."

"But—"

"No buts. My conversation with you is when I give you the time machine. Get out of here and start experimenting." He then walked over to me and pressed a button on the device he had given me—or would shortly be giving me—and he disappeared. Actually, what happened is that *I* returned to the present. It was just past noon, the empty water bottle was in the trash, and my supply of Glenfiddich had been depleted.

Okay, it was a time machine. It worked. What should I do now? I decided that what I needed to do was test the idea of making changes in time. According to Future Willy, some changes were possible and others were not, but he couldn't come up with a rule that let him determine in advance what he could or could not do. Apparently, that was a task that I was to undertake. Again I decided that attempting something simple was better than something complicated. I recalled that last Monday I had been in the department office pouring myself a cup of coffee when there was a loud noise from a lab down the hall and I was so startled I had dropped my mug and gotten hot coffee all over me. Such noises were not unusual, particularly in undergraduate classes, but timing is everything. If I had been sitting at my desk with my mug set down, it would have been no big deal. However, the noise coming just as I was pouring the coffee led to a mess and a not-inconsiderable amount of pain. My plan was to go back and figure out a way to stop myself from pouring coffee at that particular moment. I would either delay myself from fetching the coffee or otherwise prevent myself from pouring it right at that time. Surely in the larger scheme of the universe, this was the pebble in the river and not the dam.

As I recalled, I had gone over to the office around 10 A.M. So do I go to my office earlier and try to prevent myself from going for coffee? Or do I go to the department office and try to stop the actual pouring? Again, I decided to take the simpler route. I would simply prevent myself from pouring the coffee. Even if I was skeptical that it was a time-traveling me from the future asking Monday me to put down the mug, the interruption should be enough to prevent the accident from taking place. The window of opportunity was something less than a minute, so there wasn't much to do beyond stopping the act itself.

I set the coordinates and pressed the button. Nothing changed. Of course. I was in my own office at 10 A.M. last Monday, and my Monday self had already gone to the department office for coffee. I quickly hurried out the door and down the hall. I didn't think the delay would matter, as the noise had come from a classroom on this floor, and whatever had caused it would have happened after the class started. I reached the department office and could see myself inside at the coffee maker. I had just picked up the mug and was reaching for the carafe of hot coffee. All I had to do was open the door and shout something; that should, at the very least, delay my pouring the coffee until after the unexpected noise.

Easy enough. I reached for the doorknob. The door wouldn't open. What was the problem? The door didn't stick. The knob wasn't broken. Why wasn't it opening? Time was running out. I twisted and twisted at the knob, but it refused to open. I was at a loss. I did the only thing I could think of: I banged on the door. Through the glass, I could see Monday me turn around in midpour. At that moment there was a huge BANG down the hall. Inside the office, I saw myself drop the mug, which banged against the counter on its way to the floor. Hot coffee flew in every direction. I saw myself scream in pain and surprise.

Come on. Getting scalded by hot coffee was crucial to the nature of the universe? That was ridiculous. I don't know why the door didn't open, but there had to be some other reason for it. As Monday me grabbed at paper towels to sop up the coffee soaking into his/my pants, as well as what had spilled over the floor, I hit the return button on the time travel device. Obviously, I would have to rethink this.

Back in the present, I poured myself another glass from my dwindling supply of scotch, and contemplated the situation. Obviously, I had arrived too late to change the past. In order to prevent my scalding, I would have to catch myself earlier. That was easy enough. I would go back a few minutes before I arrived in the department office, so I would already be there when Monday me showed up to get the cup of coffee. Then I could simply step forward, stop myself from pouring, and however my past self reacted to my appearance, that delay should be enough.

So I set the device for ten minutes earlier last Monday, and found myself still in my office. I didn't see my past self there, but all I had to do was go down the hall and wait for my arrival in the department office. There was only one problem. My office door wouldn't open. I pulled. I banged. I did everything I could think of, but the door wouldn't open. When I looked up at the clock, it was just past ten. I had missed it again.

Okay, I thought, this really can't be that difficult. It's a cup of coffee, for crying out loud. I didn't even bother returning to the present. I set the controls for half an hour earlier. It was now forty minutes before I went for the coffee. The door to my office opened easily. I walked down the hallway to the department office. The door to that office opened easily as well. It was 9:35. In twenty-five minutes, I'd come in through that door to get my morning coffee. It wasn't even a matter of convincing myself. Although *I* now believed time travel was possible, my Monday self would not. That didn't matter. All I had to do was reveal myself and say, "Stop." I would no doubt be so baffled that I would stop whatever it was I was doing—in this case pouring a cup of coffee—and try to figure out who this person was who looked like me who was trying to prevent me from doing so. What could possibly go wrong?

Of course now I had to wait in the department office for half an hour without anyone asking me what I was doing there and why I didn't go back to my own office. So I went to my mailbox and made a big production of going through my mail. There was a memo about how to deal with snow emergencies that I was expected to share with my students. There was a catalog from an academic publisher about a new edition of their basic physics text. The odd thing was they had come out with a new edition just last year, and it wasn't like there had been these huge scientific breakthroughs that required a massive rewrite. Yet a new edition was out with the chapters completely reordered, so I couldn't just assign the same text and say "Read chapter three." Last year, chapter three was about Newtonian laws; this year, it was about quantum mechanics. Every year they would come out with a new edition, even if it only involved shuffling the chapters. It was all a scam to prevent students from simply buying used copies of earlier editions. If the professor wasn't using a text he had written himself, he was at as much of a disadvantage as the students.

It was now quarter of ten. In fifteen minutes, I'd come in to get my coffee. I was already in the office, so there was no way to keep me out. If my Monday self suddenly discovered that *he* couldn't get in, that would only serve to fulfill my purpose.

"Professor Price?"

I looked up. It was Mrs. Hammer, the department secretary. "Yes?"

"Dr. Surkis would like to see you."

"Of course," I replied. "Give me a few minutes. I'm supposed to be meeting a student here right now. I'll be in as soon as that's done."

"I'm sorry," she said. "Dr. Surkis has to leave soon for a meeting with the provost. This shouldn't take very long."

I glanced at the clock. Twelve minutes to ten. *Okay,* I thought, *let me deal with this and get it out of the way.* I followed Mrs. Hammer into the rear of the departmental suite, where the chairman had her office. "Just a moment," she said as she disappeared into the further confines of the department. I sighed. Such was the protocol in any hierarchy. If you were lower, you had to hop to when summoned, but if you were higher, you got to make underlings wait until you were ready. The clock now said nine minutes to ten. "Go on in," said Mrs. Hammer, as she stood aside so I could enter the chair's office.

Her office was strictly administrative. She did not conduct research there. In fact, as chair she was no longer required to conduct research at all. She had gone over to the other side, and only had to ride herd on those of us who were still actually laboring in the field of physics as opposed to college administration. Dr. Surkis was behind her desk talking on the phone, and she motioned me to take a seat. It was seven minutes to ten.

"All of our faculty members are doing crucial research," she was saying to whomever she was addressing. "They're on the cutting edge of their various fields, and will be bringing great honor to the university when they achieve their breakthroughs." She gave me a smile as if to say, "Look what I have to put up with." The clock was clicking closer to ten. "If you want to cut some fat out of the budget, why not look at film studies? How much money are we spending so students can watch movies?"

I indicated I could come back when this conversation was done, but she made it clear I was to remain. It was four minutes before ten.

"One member of our faculty is part of the team who has proven that the universe is expanding at an increasing rate. We're talking about a potential Nobel Prize here. Why would you want to cut our budget now?"

It was two minutes before ten. I got up and indicated I would be right back, but she insisted I stay. I couldn't believe this. It was as if the universe was conspiring to assure that I did not prevent me from spilling hot coffee all over myself.

"Look," said Dr. Surkis, "I know you were an economist, so you don't have the slightest idea what the measurement of baryon acoustic oscillations means…"

There was a sudden boom. It was just past ten. I had been prevented from stopping myself again. Clearly, I was not going to be allowed to prevent this coffee incident. I had no idea why such a trivial event was beyond my ability to prevent it, but without a doubt, this was something that had to happen. I got up and walked out of the room. Dr. Surkis could talk to my Monday self, now frantically wiping hot coffee off his pants, the counter, and the floor.

My job was to figure out what I would do next.

If my pouring coffee was such a crucial event that the universe could not allow it to be disrupted, what would be an example of something so trivial that I could easily revise the timeline?

HISTORY LESSON

"I have to admit it," said Miller, "You spin a good yarn. Maybe you should try your hand at writing science fiction yourself. I don't know that I can do much with your story, but I bet the *Star Trek* and *Doctor Who* fans would eat it up."

Price sighed. "I understand it's hard to believe—"

"Professor Price—"

"Willy, please."

"Willy, it's not hard to believe. It's impossible to believe. Even if I were to accept everything you say, what's my lead? 'Professor Wilford Price claims to have travelled in time, but revealed that he wasn't able to have an impact on anything.' Hold the presses!"

The professor rose, and Miller rose with him, hoping this meant the interview was now over, and he could finally return to planet Earth and get back to reality. No such luck. The professor pulled a cap off a hook on the back of his office door and put it atop his head. If he had a duster and a pair of goggles, he would have looked as if he was getting ready to crank up his Model T. "Max, let me take you to lunch."

It was early afternoon and the day had warmed up. It was one of those days Miller had loved when he was a student. Winter would be here soon enough—some snowfall before Thanksgiving was not unheard of—but today was a day for hanging out in a T-shirt and shorts, maybe tossing a Frisbee across the quadrangle, maybe just sitting outside and basking in the sun. There were students doing all of that and more as Miller and Price crossed in front of the library to head over to the dining hall. As they entered the building and neared the entranceway to the various food bays, Miller experienced that familiar rush of nostalgia again. He could hear the clatter of plates and silverware and trays amidst the general hubbub of conversation around the tiered dining area. Most of the tables were empty now. They had missed the height of the lunchtime rush, although the meal was still being served.

Price picked up a bowl of vegetable soup and a glass of lemonade. Miller's nostalgia didn't quite extend to institutional favorites like "American chop suey," which turned out to be today's lunch special. Instead, he got himself a turkey sandwich on rye. Over in one corner of the serving area, a sushi station was being set up for dinner time.

"Sushi? When did they start offering that?"

The professor, busily settling with the cashier for their lunches, looked up. "What? Oh, I have no idea. I don't come here very often. I just thought some food in a quiet corner of the room might be more conducive to conversation." They took their trays over to a table overlooking an open expanse of campus. Some of the older dorms and the university gym were visible through the windows, and Miller could see that the trees were in their autumn glory. It was the sort of day that yearbook photographers dream of, as they go about fixing memories for the alumni of the future.

Miller took a bite out of his sandwich. Using the horseradish dressing he had found at the condiments station instead of the mayonnaise gave the sandwich some extra zest, which broke him out of his reverie. "Thank you for lunch, Willy, but I don't know if there's much more for us to discuss," he said. "Your story is certainly amusing, but there's nothing there to back it up."

The professor broke off a piece of his roll and dipped it into his soup before plopping it into his mouth. "Ah, that's much better," he smiled. He looked up and gazed at the young reporter. "In fact there's much, much more to discuss, Max. We've barely scratched the surface. For the moment, though, I'm willing to accept that you don't believe anything I'm telling you. Can you do me the same favor in return?"

"How do you mean?" said Miller, wiping some dressing off his fingers with his napkin.

"I want you to play 'What if?' with me. You don't have to believe my story, but I want you to accept my hypothesis for the moment. You have a time machine. You discover you can't change some things, but you're told that there are other things that you can change. Where and when are you going to go? If you're going to test it, what are you going to try to change?"

Miller was suddenly taken back to those late night dorm room conversations. They might be drunk or stoned, but no one wanted to go to bed yet, and they would talk about politics or movies or music or—if they had smoked enough weed—the meaning of life. Price's question fell into this last category. The reporter took another bite of his sandwich, giving himself a few more moments in which to think. Finally he said, "Well, I suppose the classic answer is that I should go back and kill Hitler, right? The personification of evil of the last century?"

Price smiled. "Excellent. Yes, you'll stop the Holocaust, and possibly World War II altogether. Very good choice. So, *sprechen sie deutsch*?"

"Excuse me?"

"I was asking you if you're fluent in German."

"Other than *Volkswagen*, I don't speak a word of it."

"Then how do you propose to maneuver through wartime Germany? You'd be arrested as an American spy the moment you opened your mouth."

"Okay, so I go back before the war. Get to him as a child, or when he was pathetic, struggling artist."

"Same problem. You don't speak German. How do you find him? How do you get close enough to do the deed? Notice that I haven't asked if you would have the ability and the will to kill such a monster if you could. You're a 21st century American lumbering around early 20th century Germany, and the only thing you can say is the name of a car that hasn't been invented yet. How are you possibly going to accomplish the task?"

Miller couldn't argue with that. Still, he was impressed that Price had obviously given it a lot of thought. "Did you try it yourself, Willy?"

"No, but I did go to some other times and places, and realized that I had enough trouble not letting my modern colloquial English give me away. It would have been even worse if I had been trying to blend in while stumbling through another language. I got onto the *Titanic*, figuring that I could warn them about the iceberg. I realized I would need some money to bribe the maître d' in the dining room in order to get me a seat at the captain's table. I gave myself away when I asked someone where the ATM was."

"Okay, I get it. You need someone who knows the territory. So, assuming such a thing was possible, suppose we hired someone who can speak German to go after Hitler? Perhaps someone who studied early twentieth century German so he—or she—could easily blend in with the crowd. Doesn't that solve your problem?" Miller couldn't resist a little smirk. He still didn't believe in Price's time machine, but in playing along with the professor's premise, he wanted to come out on top.

The professor smiled. "Now you're thinking. That's very clever. And, of course recruiting someone for this mission would be a breeze, since there would be many people willing to kill one of the worst mass murderers in history. All we would have to do is convince them the time machine was real. Look how easily I've been able to convince you."

Price looked at him in a way suggesting that he had won, but that he wasn't happy about doing it. Of course the young man's "solution" would only work if the time machine was real and easy enough to demonstrate. Miller had to admit the academic had him there, using his own skepticism against him. Still, he wasn't willing to give up. He usually came out on top in those late night bull sessions. "Okay, let's pick something more recent. How about preventing 9/11?"

"You speak fluent Arabic?"

"No, no," said Miller, "I wouldn't try to convince the terrorists not to go. I would warn our government."

Miller couldn't have guessed the professor's reaction. Price sighed. "Yes, your instincts are absolutely right. I had the very same idea. And I can report that it worked." He seemed a bit choked up, and reached for the lemonade.

"I don't understand," said Miller. "What do you mean it worked? I was just a little kid, but I clearly remember how upset my mother was that day. She was glued to the TV set, completely broken up by it, and telling me how she would keep me safe from the evil in the world. An uncle of a friend of mine worked in the World Trade Center…"

"Yes, I know… no, not about your friend's uncle, of course, but that the attack still occurred in spite of my warnings."

"Then how can you say that your plan worked?"

"My plan did work. I managed to plant information that I knew the authorities would have to pick up. I planted it over several years. And nearly all of it got through… and was almost completely ignored. A report that terrorists wanted to crash a plane into the World Trade Center was dismissed by the FAA as 'highly unlikely.' The CIA received word that terrorists were planning to hijack commercial airliners. There was never any follow-up. The White House got repeated warnings about an 'imminent' attack by al-Qaeda. They decided it was just an attempt to distract them from the 'real threat' of Saddam Hussein and his imaginary weapons of mass destruction. No matter how many clues I planted for the authorities which pointed to Osama bin Laden planning an attack, no one took it seriously. That was the problem. Some things can be changed and some things can't, but until I tried to change them, there was no way for me to tell in advance what was immutable and what was up for negotiation."

They were both quiet for a while after that. Miller noticed they were among the handful of people left in the large dining room, but no one was chasing them out. Of course this whole exercise was merely a game of "let's pretend" as far as Miller was concerned, but the notion that the professor could have been responsible for all those red flags that had been ignored was sobering. What would it feel like to warn people of an impending disaster that you know with certainty is coming, and yet have no effect whatsoever? Miller thought of the myth of Cassandra, whose curse was that her own accurate predictions went unheeded. Whether Price was responsible for them or not, there was no doubt that the warnings had been there, and that they had had no effect whatsoever.

Miller pushed his tray with his now-empty plate aside. "You said you were able to change some things. So what did you change? Vietnam still happened. Adam Sandler still has a movie career. The Beatles never reunited. What's different? What did you actually change?"

The professor drained his lemonade glass and placed it on his own tray. "Probably the biggest historical event I affected was that I was able to stop the U.S. attack on Toronto."

The reporter stared at him across the table. In the distance, they could hear the clatter of some pots from the kitchen area. For a long moment, neither said a word. Then Miller broke the silence. "I'm sorry, it sounded like you said you stopped an attack on Toronto."

"That's right," responded Price matter-of-factly. "And it wasn't merely an attack. I helped avert a war between the United States and Canada."

"I never heard of any war between us and Canada."

"Exactly," said Price triumphantly. He was beaming.

"Do you have any proof of this?"

"Of course not. It never happened." Price paused to relish his success before continuing. "Let me explain. The country had become very bitter about international trade agreements, and we were in the midst of some very contentious negotiations with Canada. And that's when the bomb went off at the U.S. Embassy in Ottawa."

Miller didn't remember any such bomb, but Price was on a roll. "The president declared that this was an attack on American sovereignty, and that Canada had become a rogue nation. American defenses were put on high alert, and it was decided that the only way to show what the president insisted on calling 'our national resolve in defense of the homeland' was to launch an immediate attack on Toronto. The British denounced this as an assault on the Commonwealth, and sent their own military forces over in support of Canada. A national draft was reinstated, and those students who hadn't been called up immediately left school to get further away from the border."

The reporter picked up Price's empty glass and took a sniff. No alcohol. Just lemonade. "Willy, that's insane."

"Yes, it was. Especially when the big sticking point in the trade negotiations was setting a price for maple syrup. Apparently American and Canadian producers could only agree on one thing: stiff tariffs on imports from the other country. When I saw that neither side was backing down, I knew I had to try to do something. Fortunately, Canadian authorities proved to be much more open to reason."

"Reason?"

"I gathered all the information I could about the bombing of the embassy and who was responsible, and then I backtracked. I dropped in and out of time over several months prior to the incident, leaving word in various places about the crackpot responsible for the attack. It turned out to be some American who had moved to Canada so that he could finally get health care he could afford. Unfortunately, his mental instability hadn't been diagnosed. Thanks to my tips in the right ears, he was arrested when he attempted to buy some explosives from an undercover agent of the CSIS, the Canadian version of the FBI. Since there was no bombing, there was no war. It turned out that the event that Time wouldn't allow to be changed wasn't the shooting war, but the trade war. I like pancakes and waffles as much as the next person, but I didn't think they were worth dying for. Time apparently agreed. What was important to preserve was the free flow of maple syrup. That was what mattered, and that was what couldn't be altered. The military action was a sideshow. What I learned was that there was just no telling in advance what the rules were, what Time considered immutable and what things could be changed or tossed aside like a used tissue."

Miller sat back in amazement. He didn't believe a word of it, but Price was certainly able to sell a story. "That would be incredible… if it was true," said Miller.

The professor stood up and took his tray over to a rack by the entranceway. Miller followed suit. "Okay, you want proof? I think you're entitled to some proof. Come with me."

The two of them left the dining hall and wended their way to the connecting tunnels that would, if the right path were followed, eventually lead them back to the physics building. However, that wasn't where Price led them. Instead, they turned off at a doorway that led to a staircase up to the library, to the main hall. In addition to the circulation desk and banks of computers, it was also the library's exhibition area. Currently on display was some sort of historical exhibit about the American theater. Price led Miller to one of the cases and pointed to a poster that showed its age both in the browning of the paper and its use of a typeface which was somewhat different from what the young man was used to seeing.

Miller was getting ready to scream at the absurdity of the situation, but they were in a library, and certain habits become ingrained. Quietly, the frustrated reporter said to the professor, "What does this have to do with anything?"

Price pointed to a small card in the case. "From the collection of Professor Wilford Price, on permanent loan," said the reporter as he read the card aloud. He then looked up to take in the entire display. What was being showcased was a poster and tickets for a benefit performance of *Our American Cousin* at Ford's Theatre in Washington, D.C., on the evening of April 14, 1865.

"Let me tell you how I tried to stop the assassination of Abraham Lincoln," said the professor. He wasn't smiling.

NOT SO SECRET SERVICE

Of course you can't just go and tell the president of the United States he shouldn't do something. This was going to require a good deal of research and preparation. Fortunately, I didn't have to learn another language. In fact, the first thing I had to do was get some period clothing. I couldn't go in my regular clothes. Even an everyday suit and tie wouldn't do. I don't pay much attention to such things, but I know that the wrong lapel or collar size would immediately make me stand out, and that's precisely what I didn't want to do.

As it turns out, I have a cousin who is one of those "re-enactors" of the Civil War. I have no idea what it is he does, but I knew he'd know where I could get clothing that would look authentic. I think I told him I needed it for a masquerade or some such thing. He put me in touch with a costume supply house, and I managed to get completely outfitted including boots. Washington in 1865 may have had sidewalks, but the streets were dirt roads used by horses. What sort of mess you stepped into depended on both the weather and the time of day, but it was going to be a mess regardless. Finally, fully dressed as I imagined a 19th century academic might look, I went back to April 11, 1865.

I'd been to Washington several times, so some of it was very familiar to me, but many of the office buildings and monuments that I knew had yet to be built. The White House and the Capitol were there, but there was no Pentagon, no Kennedy Center and, of course, no Lincoln Memorial. It would have been interesting to go and explore the city, but I wasn't there as a tourist. I was going to bring the details of John Wilkes Booth's plan and that of his co-conspirators to the attention of someone who could get it to Lincoln. That ought to be enough to either lead to Lincoln changing his plans or authorities rounding up Booth and his gang. My experience in Toronto had shown me that having a mass of convincing evidence would be the most likely way to get someone's attention.

I got a room at the National Hotel on the corner of Pennsylvania Avenue and Sixth Street. It was where Booth was staying, and it was just a few blocks from the Capitol, which I could see off in the distance. I had brought my notebook with my handwritten notes, since my laptop would be utterly useless in this era. Even with a few hours on its battery, there would be no way to recharge it, and if I had asked about Wi-Fi, they would have thought I was talking Chinese. Instead what I brought was a detailed account in writing that covered Booth's movements three days hence.

There was a relaxed mood in Washington. Lee had surrendered to Grant two days before, and the four long bloody years of war had finally come to an end. Somewhere in the city President Lincoln and his men, as well as Congressional leaders, were starting to come to grips with that fact, and were now considering how—or whether—the southern rebels would be reintegrated into society. Grant had let the southern soldiers go home with their horses and small arms, and even fed them before they left. A few weeks ago, a strange man such as myself wandering around the city taking notes might have aroused suspicions, since the capital had been a target of the Confederate forces. But now people simply hurried about their business, focused on the future and perhaps awaiting word about their own family members in uniform.

I was sitting in the lobby of the hotel late in the day when I spotted Booth. He cut a dashing figure in his tailored clothes complete with silk hat and kid gloves. He was an actor and a star, which made him something of a celebrity. He nodded in acknowledgment to people who recognized him as he crossed the lobby and exited the hotel. I decided to follow him. He went over to Ford's Theater, which was where I knew he received his mail while he was in town. I waited outside, watching the horse drawn carriages go by and trying not to get ill from the horses relieving themselves in the street. I don't how those people put up with it. The stench made my eyes water. However they'd probably have the same reaction if they found themselves walking down a city street in the 21st century and had to smell the auto exhaust. Humans seem to be able to get used to anything.

Booth was joined by a friend, and they started walking and talking. I stayed sufficiently behind so that I wouldn't call attention to myself, but it also meant I couldn't follow their conversation. I had no idea where we were heading when suddenly I saw a very familiar landmark. We were going to the White House.

There was no Secret Service back then. I later learned that it wouldn't even be formed until that July, and it would be years before protecting the president and his family became one of their main purposes. Instead, there was an Army sentry who was letting people onto the grounds without even patting them down for concealed weapons. There was a large crowd milling about, but suddenly it got very quiet. I looked in the same direction as everyone else, and then I saw him. It was Abraham Lincoln, large as life, and looking somewhat weary. It's become commonplace to note that the presidency ages those who hold office. I had little idea of what Lincoln looked like when he assumed the job a few years earlier, but it was clear to me that this was a man who had been carrying a heavy load. As the president began to speak, I tried to get closer to Booth and his friend.

Lincoln's address was about the war ending, and how he intended to deal with the rebel states. There was a lot in his speech that I didn't quite follow, focusing on Louisiana for some reason, but there was no question that this was a man used to commanding the attention of his audience. It was equally obvious that his listeners had much longer attention spans than my students.

"We all agree that the seceded States, so called, are out of their proper relation with the Union; and that the sole object of the government, civil and military, in regard to those States is to again get them into that proper practical relation. I believe it is not only possible, but in fact, easier to do this, without deciding, or even considering, whether these States have ever been out of the Union, than with it," he said. "Finding themselves safely at home, it would be utterly immaterial whether they had ever been abroad. Let us all join in doing the acts necessary to restoring the proper practical relations between these States and the Union; and each forever after, innocently indulge his own opinion whether, in doing the acts, he brought the States from without, into the Union, or only gave them proper assistance, they never having been out of it."

Lincoln then turned his attention back to Louisiana, which was apparently the issue of the day. The legislature there had acted to abolish slavery, extending the vote and opening the schools to newly freed slaves. Apparently some thought this went too far, and were urging the government not to recognize Louisiana's actions, but Lincoln was having none of it. If he rejected what Louisiana had done as a condition of bringing them back into the fold, he said, it would send the wrong message. "Now, if we reject, and spurn them, we do our utmost to disorganize and disperse them. We in effect say to the white men 'You are worthless, or worse—we will neither help you, nor be helped by you.' To the blacks we say 'This cup of liberty which these, your old masters, hold to your lips, we will dash from you, and leave you to the chances of gathering the spilled and scattered contents in some vague and undefined when, where, and how.'"

It all seemed a bit verbose to me but when I glanced at Booth, I could see the fire in his eyes. Lincoln's words had enraged him, and I heard him mutter darkly about citizenship for blacks, although that was not the word he used. I moved a bit closer and heard him quietly vow, "That is the last speech he will ever make."

In my hotel room that night, I gathered all my notes and maps and diagrams. Booth planned to do more than murder President Lincoln. Other members of his team were targeting Vice President Andrew Johnson and Secretary of State William Seward. They intended to decapitate the Union government and derail the plans for Reconstruction. I had all the details and didn't really need to do any further research, but I wanted to have some sense of actually living in the time before trying to change it.

On Wednesday afternoon, I made my way back to the White House. I had a satchel with me filled with all my detailed information. Now I had to get it to someone. I could have tried to speak to Lincoln himself, I suppose. I actually gave that some thought. I mean, who wouldn't want the opportunity to meet one of the greatest men in American history? The odd thing was, I might have been able to do it. Just as I had easily gotten in to hear Lincoln's speech the night before, there was little stopping me from going into the White House itself and waiting patiently with others who were hoping to catch the president's eye and ear, many clutching fistfuls of papers or other material, presumably supporting their various claims. Even if I had been fortunate enough to speak with him, though, it didn't seem likely I could convince him that his life was at risk if he went to the theater that evening.

Instead, I went up to a man at a desk who seemed to be trying—and failing—to bring order to the chaos in the hallway. "No," he was saying to a matronly woman who seemed to be on the verge of tears, "We can't track down your son right now. We have nearly a million men in uniform.

The war is over. If your son is alive, he will get word to you and no doubt come home safely." That wasn't the answer she was looking for, but the man turned his attention to me as a way of letting her know she had been dismissed. "And what business do you have with the president?"

"Actually, I don't want to see the president. I wish to see William Crook."

This seemed to startle the man. "Crook? The president's bodyguard? Is this official business? Is he expecting you?" He gave me the fish eye. "I don't know what this is all about, but don't think you can use him as a back door to getting your plea to President Lincoln."

In fact, that was precisely what I was planning. "No, he's not expecting me, but I have some information that will be vital to him. Ask him if he can spare a few moments for Professor Price." My name, of course, was meaningless to this functionary, but the title managed to have the desired effect.

"I don't think he's on duty yet, but I did see him come in. Try that office on the right at the end of the hall."

Thanking the man, I worked my way through the throng and out the other side. Crook was a member of the Washington police force who had become one of Lincoln's bodyguards in January. The president had taken a great interest in the young man. When Crook was threatened with being recalled to active military duty, Lincoln interceded on his behalf to keep him stationed at the White House and, not incidentally, home with his wife and young boy. In fact, it was to Crook that Lincoln observed that if someone wanted to kill him, there wasn't much anyone could do about it, even if Crook and the other guards took down the assassin. I hoped to prove him wrong.

It wasn't so much an office as a large walk-in closet. Uniforms and changes of clothes were hung on a rack. Some crates were stacked against one wall. An open box on the floor was half-filled with ammunition. This was apparently the staging area for the White House bodyguards. Crook was in his shirtsleeves at a small table wedged into a corner, where he was meticulously cleaning his gun. He looked up in surprise.

"You've got the wrong office, sir. This area is closed to the public."

I entered the room and closed the door behind me. Crook started to rise, and I raised my hands to indicate I was no threat to him. Although I was only a few years older than him, I had no doubt that we both quickly

assassination of Lincoln, someone at the hotel remembered the man who kept inquiring as to the vice president's whereabouts, and it was only a matter of time before he was picked up.

Crook's diligence was noted, and he went on to a long and honored career. As Colonel Crook, he was given the title of "disbursing agent of the White House" by President Ulysses S. Grant, a post which he held until his retirement many years later. Had he been able to convince President Lincoln to heed my warning, he might yet be remembered as one of the greatest heroes of American history.

FUTURE TENSE

It was after three as the professor and the reporter made their way out of the library and onto the quadrangle. It was still warm, but there was a hint of a chill breeze in the air. The sun had started its descent toward the western horizon.

"There'll be frost on the pumpkins tonight," said Price.

"Pardon?"

"Something my mother used to say."

The reporter looked at him. They were in front of the physics building, and he had no desire to go back inside. This story was clearly going nowhere. It might have made for an interesting movie if one liked such things, but there was no news to report. "Professor Price—Willy—I want to thank you for your time. I really should be getting back to the office now…"

The professor smiled ruefully. "I understand it's going to take a lot more convincing."

"Really, I think you've told me what I need…" The reporter's demurral was cut short by the beeping of his cell phone. He pulled it out of his pocket and silenced it without looking.

"I think you may want to take this message."

Miller looked quizzically at the professor, but then looked down at the screen. He had an incoming text message. He performed the gestures that an earlier generation might have thought were magical to make the message appear on the screen. He looked at it and gave a start. Then he looked at Price. Then he looked at the screen again. Finally he glared at the professor, clearly annoyed. "You want to tell me how you did that?"

"Did what?" answered Price, all innocence.

The reporter held up the screen. "This." On the screen was a message: "Don't cut the interview short. The good stuff is coming." That wasn't what set him off. It was the signature: "Max." Miller checked the incoming calls log and saw that the message was recorded as coming from his own phone. "I obviously didn't send this message to myself."

Price shrugged. "According to your phone, it's obvious that you did. Check the time stamp."

Miller looked at when the text had been sent. It was a minute ago, when he was talking to the professor and certainly wasn't sending any messages to himself or anyone else. So either someone had spoofed his own phone to make it appear he was texting himself, or else…

The professor smiled. This just seemed to get Miller more worked up. "No, Willy, that's impossible. There's something wrong here."

"Max, most people—including yourself—would say that my story is impossible. What you just experienced was a moment of doubt, of uncertainty. Is this real or not? I promise you I did not send that text to your phone. And if you're startled by that uncertainty, that not knowing the whole story, then you need to hear the rest of mine."

Miller felt dazed. "I don't know what to believe, but I may as well see this through to the end," he said as he slipped the phone back into his pocket.

They were back in the cluttered office on the third floor. The noise from the hallway was more subdued. Late afternoon classes were getting underway, but many of the professors—and students—tried to arrange schedules that allowed them to work on their own projects late in the day. Price pulled out a bottle labeled "The Balvenie"—complete with the definite article—and two glasses from his bottom drawer.

"This is going to take a while, and we may not want to be driving after a dram or two. Would you like me to order in, or should we get a cab to take us to some quiet restaurant?"

Miller sipped the amber liquid Price proffered. "I wasn't really planning on making a day of this. How much more of the story is there to go?"

"We've barely scratched the surface. Would you prefer to come back tomorrow? I can call your editor…"

"No, no, no," replied Miller quickly. "Let's get this done today."

"As you wish," said Price. "This shouldn't take too long." He spent just a few minutes on the phone ordering a taxi to pick them up in three hours, and called a restaurant where he seemed to be confirming a reservation that he had previously made. The reporter noted he hadn't had to look up either number, but wasn't sure what to make of that. Perhaps the old academic regularly needed assistance to get home, and the restaurant was a favorite haunt.

When Price hung up the phone, he picked up his own glass and gestured a toast to the reporter. "I appreciate your taking the time to hear me out."

Miller raised his glass in salute. "There's a zoning hearing tonight," he sighed. "I won't be losing sleep over missing it." The smooth single malt was having its effect.

Price refilled their glasses. "So let me continue. I returned from the 19th century somewhat disillusioned. Apparently Lincoln's death was one of those events that Time required to occur. You won't be surprised to learn that I have yet to discover the secret of what can be changed and what can't. After all, my future self hadn't uncovered it himself, so I could hardly be expected to do so."

Miller put his cellphone back on the desk. He might as well continue recording the interview, he thought. It was either leading to a great story, or evidence for a sanity hearing. "So what did you do next?"

"The past was a frustrating mystery," said the professor. "I decided I would go into the future instead."

"Okay, that makes sense. Or, at least, it makes as much sense as anything else you've told me. So where did you go? Off to the far future to see the Morlocks and Eloi?"

"No, I went to 2004."

"To see the Red Sox?"

Price laughed. "No, I have no interest in baseball. However, my future self had been able to tell me that the Red Sox would break their 86-year-old losing streak, and I wanted to see if it was true. As you probably know, it was. I then went back to April of 2004 and placed money with several Las Vegas odds makers on the Red Sox winning the series."

Miller had evidently decided to just go with the flow. "Okay, I'll bite. Why Las Vegas? Why not just place your bet with a local bookie?"

The professor leaned back in his chair and smiled. "As if I would know how to find a local bookie. This is where age and cunning has it over youth and daring. First of all, I wanted to spread my money around so as to not call attention to myself. Betting on the Red Sox to win the Series was apparently something that was considered bizarre, but you can't discount sentiment. I placed $5,000 with one establishment, and was told that someone had already bet $20,000 on the Chicago Cubs. The difference, of course, was that I already knew the outcome."

Miller pondered that as he took another sip. "Okay, but why did you place several bets? Since you knew it was a sure thing, you really only had to place one."

Price slapped his palm down on his desk. "Precisely. And if I had put all my money down on a single long-shot bet, don't you think it would have called attention to me? That's what I was trying to avoid. By spreading it around—I made fifteen separate wagers—I was simply an eccentric Red Sox fan, not someone trying to beat the system. As it was, once I collected my winnings that October, I beat a hasty retreat back to my own time. I was not interested in dealing with anyone suspicious about my winnings. And that's where I faced a different problem."

"Let me guess. Las Vegas had time machines as well."

"No," said Price, "but they had something just as troublesome: the Treasury Department. In 1996, they started redesigning the currency. I couldn't bring a 2004 fifty dollar bill into a bank in 1999. Not only wouldn't they have accepted it, but I might have been arrested for counterfeiting, although the newer bills looked so different they might have questioned my sanity rather than my honesty."

"So you couldn't spend it?"

"What I had to do was go through my winnings bill by bill. The ones that were good in 1999 got deposited in my bank account. Bills that wouldn't start circulating until 2000 or 2003 or 2004 were put aside. Of course, with the time machine, I simply had to pop into my bank in those years with the appropriate bills. I began constantly going through not only my paper money, but my coins and even my credit cards. I had to constantly be on the lookout for the dates on them, whether for minting or expiration. Fortunately, once the money was in the account, I could draw it out subsequent to that time in what would be the current currency."

If one accepted Price's absurd premise that he had a working time machine, this all made perfect sense, thought Miller. However, the obvious flaw in the plan wouldn't go away. "Okay, you make this sports bet and cash in and make a lot of money. Great. Why didn't you really cash in by checking out the stock market? You could have invested in Enron before they tanked, or in Amazon or even Microsoft as start-ups…"

"One would think," said Price. "What I found was that attempts to go into the past and call a broker led me into the same dead end as trying to stop me scalding myself with hot coffee. And going into the future to get such information proved impossible."

Miller was getting a bit slap happy at this point, but held out his glass for a refill just the same. "Let me get this straight. You could bet on the Red Sox, but not the stock market?"

Price poured a bit more into both their glasses, then closed the bottle and returned it to his drawer. "I think we should stay sober enough to be able to walk into the restaurant on our own," he said with a wry chuckle. "And, yes, apparently sports bets are made in so many locations that someone with future information doesn't upset the system, as long as one doesn't get greedy. I don't know what would have happened if I had taken all my Red Sox winnings to 2025."

"What happens in 2025?"

"It seems I'm not allowed to say. However, what I've been able to figure out is that while sports bets are okay—at least when they're widely dispersed—the stock market is not. If one tried to buy up a substantial portion of, say, Apple when it went public in 1980, it would have seriously distorted the time stream. Believe me, I know. I tried."

"Okay, you can't change the past in that regard, but what's to prevent you from going into the future, finding out what tomorrow's hot properties are, and buying them today?"

Price drained his glass. "The future's not what it used to be, my boy. I learned that the hard way."

STOP SIGN

If the past had been frustrating, the future looked to be promising. Most of the things I had tried to change in the past had ended in defeat. Averting a war was no small thing, but the attempts to try to change the past proved psychologically debilitating as much as anything else. How many failures is a man supposed to swallow in the hopes that the *next* time will be successful? After a while, it just gets on your nerves. It would be one thing if I had a working hypothesis. Then, at least, I would be testing it and revising it in the face of new results (or non-results). However, what I was doing was tantamount to throwing darts while blindfolded, hoping that sooner or later I might actually hit a target.

Instead, I decided to change tactics and go into the future. My initial forays to bet on the 2004 Boston Red Sox had been successful. As a result, I now had enough money put away so that financial issues would no longer a problem for me, at least in the short term. Of course, some of that money would take a few years to arrive in my account, but there was enough 1999 currency to cover my immediate needs. It occurred to me that if I knew of other surefire investments, I could increase that cushion. It's not like I was getting greedy. My needs are relatively simple. However, padding the margin for error certainly couldn't hurt.

Initially, I tried to go backwards and invest early in those things I knew would pay off, but I quickly learned that wasn't allowed. It was like playing pinball. You could bang the machine a bit, but if you tried too much, it went "Tilt!" So the obvious thing for me to do was to go in the opposite direction. I decided I would go several years into the future, give or take, and learn what the hot commodities on Wall Street would be in the future. Then I could return to my time and invest in them before they got hot. It made perfect sense. So I set the device for forty years into the future and planned to spend a few hours doing research.

I pressed the button, and there was a brief flicker. I was still in what was clearly my office. Apparently that wasn't going to change. I had hoped that I would be department chairman or an honored scholar *emeritus*, but clearly this was still *my* office. I couldn't believe that I had somehow failed to get tenure. I had dutifully researched, published, and even won obscure honors that would impress the tenure committee, although no one else might know about them. If I had been rejected, I probably would have left the university to start again elsewhere. So, I guessed this office was the best I was going to get. I checked the bottom drawer of my desk. There was a bottle of an 18-year-old Glenmorangie there, so I seemed to be doing okay.

All right then. Off to the library.

I went through the main entrance of the library and it seemed utterly familiar. Why shouldn't it? The building had opened in 1930, and even with the extension in 1969 and the various upgrades for computers over the years, it was still a classic academic building. I stepped through the detectors by the entranceway, not worrying about them since they were there to catch anyone trying to remove—by design or forgetfulness—any library material. No sooner was I though them, though, than two uniformed security guards came up to me.

They were both young men, one looking decidedly more callow than the other. The older of the two said, "Could you please come with us and answer a few questions?"

Not wanting to make a scene, I accompanied them into a small office just beyond the front lobby. We walked down a hallway to the left of and behind the circulation desk. I had never been here before, but then I was rarely approached by anyone on the occasions I had needed to use the library.

We stepped into a non-descript room which seemed utterly devoid of any personality. There was a desk and some chairs. A calendar was hanging on the wall. A computer work station was situated on the desk. There was a filing cabinet in the corner. Yet I got the distinct impression that no one was actually using this space. I turned to face the young men and one of them, apparently the junior of the pair, pulled out some sort of device. He pointed it at me and started to raise and lower it as if scanning me, all the while staring at a screen attached to it.

"He's definitely a traveler. At least thirty years out of his time frame," he reported to the other.

"Well, what do you have to say for yourself?" said the older of the two although, if I had to guess, there was barely three years between them.

"I'm sorry. Who are you? What seems to be the problem?"

"Look, we know you've got a time travel device and you're from the past. We're here to make sure that you don't access any information that isn't permitted."

He seemed very certain of his authority. Nonetheless, I decided to challenge him. "I'm a member of the faculty doing some research. I don't have to answer to you or anyone else."

The younger one piped up. "I think he's a newbie."

"Shh," said the older one to his partner. He then turned back to me. "Look, you're welcome to wander around campus, but the library is off-limits. You're also forbidden from accessing any computers or attempting to solicit information from anyone in this time frame."

"And under whose authority are you giving me orders? Campus security does not get to instruct professors as to what they may research."

The younger one spoke up again. "Is this your first trip to the future?"

I decided to play dumb. "I don't know what you're talking about."

The older one attempted to regain control of the situation. "Look, there's no use denying it. We know you're from at least thirty years ago, and you are *not* allowed to use the library. People are not permitted to go back to their own time frames with future knowledge."

"And don't try accessing the Meganet on your own," added the younger one, clearly eager to assert his own authority as well.

"The Meganet?"

"Be quiet," said the older guard to his companion. He turned back to me. "He meant the Infranet. You're not allowed to do any research in this time frame."

"Do you mean the Internet?"

The younger one turned on his partner. "See? You don't know everything either."

The two of them seemed at a loss, and I thought that I might assert my own authority. "I don't know what you're going on about. I'm a member of the faculty and my access to library materials is without question." I made to move to the door, but the older one blocked my way.

"I guess you are a newbie. Let me explain. Access to library materials is only given to people in this time frame or from the future. People from the past are barred because it might disrupt the temporal flow."

I took a long, hard look at him, and I saw him backing down just a bit. Maybe I could bluff my way through. "You really don't know what you're talking about, do you?"

The younger one spoke up again. "Look, mister or professor or whatever you are, we're just two work study students. This is our job. Anyone who sets off the temporal alarm is not permitted in the library. I'm sorry, but I'm not going to screw up my financial aid and let you in. I need this job."

I couldn't quite believe what I was hearing, but it was fascinating nonetheless. "So, let me get this straight. You've been getting a lot of time travelers from the past? Is that why they have to hire guards?"

"Don't answer that!" shouted the older one before the younger one could reply. "We're not authorized to answer your questions or discuss any issues. All we can do is prevent you from entering the library."

It was clear that these two really didn't know what they were doing, and were simply following their basic instructions. "What would happen if I simply ignored you and walked out that door? Or went back to my own time, went to the part of the library I wanted to access, and came forward again?"

The younger one gave me a wide-eyed look. "You don't want to try that. I saw what they did to the last guy who did it, and it wasn't pretty."

"Quiet!" demanded his partner. "This conversation is over. You may wander the campus if you wish, so long as you abide by the rules. Otherwise, go back to your own time. You will not be permitted to gain any information here."

This was obviously an exercise in futility. I pulled out the time travel device, and they made no attempt to stop me. Instead of hitting "return," I set it for an hour into the future. When I made the transition, they were still there.

"Really," said the older one, "do you imagine you're the first person to try that?"

They then firmly escorted me back out through the lobby and out the front door. Once I was back outside, they stood by the door, blocking my way. "And don't try the other entrances," said the younger one. "We've got guards everywhere."

"Be quiet!" yelled his partner. They continued to bicker as I walked across the quad back to my office.

It seems some sort of time travel bureaucracy had developed, and they were not going to be helpful. It's not like this was of any concern to me. I simply had to figure out a way to do an end run around them. Returning to my office, I decided that I hadn't gone far enough into the future. I could go a couple of centuries ahead and simply look back at what stocks had gone up over the decade in front of me. I wasn't trying to assure income for my descendants for all time, after all. It didn't really matter *when* the information came from, so long as it was helpful to me when I got back to my own time.

So, setting my coordinates for another one hundred and fifty years into the future, I pressed the button, hoping I would no longer have to deal with literal minded work study students. I didn't know who would have this office in two centuries—presumably long after my retirement and (I had to assume) death—but I would have to hope they were not around when I popped into their time. I suppose I could have shifted what time of day I arrived, but there was no guarantee the office would be empty. Nearly two hundred years from my time? Who knew when professors would show up on campus, if they even showed up at all?

Not knowing what to expect, I hit the button. To my amazement, my office disappeared and was replaced by... nothing.

I was in some sort of gray limbo. I could vaguely smell something that reminded me of the ocean, but there was no body of water to be seen. In fact, there was nothing to be seen. In every direction I looked, there was nothing but gray. It wasn't like being in a fog. There was no sense of distance, of any depth or height. It was simply... nothing.

"Hello, there!"

From off in the distance—or not—a man approached. He was bald with a crown of white hair, and an equally white beard and moustache. In spite of this appearance of great age, he seemed quite youthful. He wasn't merely non-threatening. He seemed to be smiling. Indeed, he looked downright jovial.

"Hello," I responded politely.

"You're obviously way out of your time," he said with a friendly air. "Is this the first trip for you?"

He was now next to me, although I couldn't say for sure I had seen or heard him traverse the distance. He held out his hand. "I'm Cort. I'm here to get you back on track. And you are?"

We shook hands. "Wilford. Where am I exactly, Mr. Cort?"

"Not Mr. Cort, Wilford. Just Cort. We're in temporal limbo. Apparently, you've travelled too far into your future. You should have read the manual more closely."

Cort was in a coarse brown robe. He reminded me of a monk. "I don't understand. What do you mean 'too far?'"

Cort sighed. "You folks really need to read the manual before you start playing with your time devices. There's a limit to how far in the future you can go, just like there's a limit to what you're able to learn about the future. Didn't you read the section on the Price Principles at all?"

"The Price Principles? I don't understand."

Cort sat down in a chair that I would have sworn hadn't been there a moment before, and motioned me to take the equally newly arrived seat beside him. "Tell me, Wilford, do you fire weapons or operate your vehicle or give birth without reading the instructions first? Why do people think that they don't need to spend time learning the rules of time travel?"

"I'm afraid my device didn't come with any manual."

"Did you get it second hand?"

"You might say that."

Cort sighed. "All right, let me explain. According to the Price Principles, you're allowed to travel wherever you want in the past with certain restrictions, but future travel becomes more and more limited the further you go. Once you get beyond your own timeline, you quickly reach a point where the future is closed to you."

"Because it costs too much?"

Cort looked surprised. "Costs?"

"You call them the Price Principles. I gather it becomes more expensive to travel as you go further into the future. Probably something to do with the conservation of energy…"

"No, no," said Cort. "It's named for the genius who discovered them, the father of time travel, Wilford Price. You must know this. You were presumably named for him."

I took a moment to absorb this, and then quietly answered, "Actually, this is all news to me. You see, I *am* Wilford Price."

Cort looked at me for a good long moment. He seemed to be studying my face. Suddenly, he gasped. "Oh my goodness, is it really you? Is this the famous 'first encounter' with time limits that you wrote about in your memoirs? I can't believe that *I'm* the one you meet." He leapt out of the seat and seemed to be dancing around. "Have I said too much? I had assumed that you were simply another traveler off the beaten time path. I had no idea…"

"Calm down, Cort. It's fine. I'm not going anywhere, and you haven't really told me anything except that I can't travel too far into the future. Why can't I?"

"Well, as the Price Principles firmly state… Oh, wait, look who I'm trying to tell. *You're* the one who discovered the limits. You should be telling me."

"Cort, please sit down. I've never done this before. This is all new to me. What can you tell me?"

The older man sat back down looking a bit flushed. "I really can't tell you anything. I probably should have sent you back immediately. But this is just too exciting. I've been studying you since I first became interested in temporal studies. You're in the pantheon with Fulton and Edison and Leibowitz…"

I couldn't quite believe what I was hearing. "Really? Who's Leibowitz?"

"Oh, I probably should haven't said that either. I think she's ahead of your time. Look, Professor Price…"

"Please, call me Willy."

"Oh my, oh my. Call you Willy. I can't believe this. I even got to play you in a pageant when I was a little boy.…"

"Cort, get a grip." The older man seemed to be beside himself. "I need your help. You have to explain what's going on here."

Cort stopped babbling and took a deep breath. "Professor—um, Willy— I'm really not allowed to tell you anything. You've travelled too far into the future, and as you proved in your definitive treatise on the subject, that's one of the iron laws of time travel. There's a limit to how far you can go."

I smiled. I liked the sound of "definitive treatise." If I still needed to qualify for tenure by then, that ought to do it for me. I patted Cort on the knee, "And when do I write this treatise proving all this?"

"Not until you're ninety.… Oh, you've got me doing it again. Willy, you really have to go back. This era and everything ahead of us is closed off to you, and I really shouldn't be telling you anything more. Not even that you're one of the greatest scientific minds who ever lived."

"Well, I don't know about that...."

"Please, Willy, this is a tremendous honor for me, and I can't wait to get home to tell the spousal collective, but you really have to return home now."

"Spousal collective?"

Cort assumed the expression of someone in a state of panic. "Please, Willy, the very structure of the space-time continuum is in danger of collapsing in upon itself."

I looked hard at him. "Really?"

His shoulders slumped. "No, not really. We're just supposed to say that to get the people who've gone too far to go back without delay. Honestly, if it was up to me, I would take you around and show you the world you helped bring into being, but as you proved so long ago, that just isn't possible."

"Well, if I said so..."

Cort looked crestfallen.

"It's okay, Cort, I know you're just doing your job. Moses didn't get to enter the Promised Land, either."

"Thank you, Willy. This is a day I'll never forget. In fact, when I'm identified as the guardian you met, I'll go down in history as well, even if it's only a footnote to your amazing life."

I embraced Cort. "I'm sure you'll do my memory justice. I'm pleased to have met you as well." I pulled the device out of my pocket and prepared to head back. Cort looked like he had something more to say. "Yes?"

He seemed embarrassed, and had to clear his throat. At last he looked up at me. "Willy, before you go, could I please have your autograph?"

THE METER IS RUNNING

Price and Miller left the quad and headed to the back of the library. It wasn't easy for cars to navigate the campus, but the "Intercampus Road" went right by the library, making it the obvious place for shuttle buses, taxis, and anyone else doing on-campus pick-ups. The sun had set, but the temperature was mild, even though both men were glad they had worn jackets.

The reporter had long given up trying to escape. The professor was an engaging companion and storyteller, and it would be easier to tell his editor there was no story if he could honestly say he had devoted hours to hearing the old codger out. Besides, he had grown curious as to what the payoff would be. Clearly Price's tale had some goal in mind, even if Miller had not yet been able to figure it out.

Students went by them, heading to evening classes or back to their dorms or the dining halls. Miller felt that pang of nostalgia again. He really had enjoyed his college days and that, more than anything, was what kept him listening to Price's preposterous stories. It was a chance to once again hang out in the place of his youth, even if that wasn't all that many years ago. College, after all, was a place where one had most of the privileges of adulthood and very few of the responsibilities. Who wouldn't want to stay there forever if one could?

Price looked down the road to see if their cab was coming, but evidently they would have a wait. Miller broke the silence. "Just to recap, if I may. You got this time machine, went into the past, and found there wasn't much could do. You went into the future and found not only that there wasn't much you could do, but there was even less you could see. I'm kind of at a loss to understand why anyone would want such a device. Once you get beyond the novelty value, it seems pretty useless, unless you have a hot sports tip."

Not seeing their cab, Price turned to the reporter. "Fair enough. And that thought is certainly what was running through my mind. What was the point of it all? Why had I bothered to go through the motions of going back in time to give my younger self a time machine, if I would be stymied at every turn?"

Miller said nothing. One of the things he had learned as a reporter is that when your interview subject starts asking himself the questions you were going to ask—particularly if they were the sorts of questions you expected him to evade—then let him do so. This was different from him trying to prompt Miller, as he had done earlier in the day. Now he was prompting himself. However, before the professor could continue his interrogation, they were distracted by some students exiting the library.

"I can't believe I got a B on the sociology midterm," complained of a gaggle heading up the hill toward the dorms. "The social sciences aren't even real science. It's such a meatball subject!"

"You're acing astronomy and physics," replied his friend. "I don't think MIT is going to care how you did in the courses you took to meet the distribution requirement."

Their voices faded out as they headed up the hill. Price smiled, "Ah, youth."

Miller tried to bring him back to the topic at hand. "So, when you saw that time travel led nowhere, what did you do?"

Price came out of his own reverie and looked at Miller. "Oh, no, no, no. I didn't say it led nowhere. I said I had been following the wrong paths."

Miller almost wished there had been a story here. At this point, he would have put in for bonus pay for what it was taking to get Price to get to the point. It had been hours, and Miller was under the impression that Price was only now starting to get warmed up. "Fine," he said. "What was the right path?"

"That's exactly the question I had," said Price with a smile. "Going to change history hadn't done me much good. Going to glean inside information about the future turned out to be barred. So what was it good for?"

At that moment, the taxi pulled up to the curb. Price gave the driver the name of the restaurant. Miller didn't recognize it. It was out of his price range and, after all, the professor had said he had money to burn. Might as well get a decent meal beyond the cafeteria sandwich he had had for lunch, thought Miller. It wasn't like anything else was going to come out of the day's effort.

As the driver took them away from the campus, Price picked up the conversation where he had left off. "So, my task was to figure out if there was some other use to which I could put the device that I had so far been ignoring. And then it came to me."

"What did?"

"I could explore my own past."

As the cab drove through the dark streets between the university and downtown, Miller wondered if even a fancy dinner was worth it. It wasn't like he could hop out of the moving taxi, though, so he had no choice but to continue. "So what did you do? Revisit your childhood?"

"No," the professor said, "An old man hanging around a schoolyard? They would have locked me up. I had a very different agenda. My father had passed away when I was just three. I never really knew him."

Of all the things Price could have said, that was the thing that resonated with Miller. "I never knew my father, either."

Price had a wistful look on his face. "It's not easy growing up without a father, is it? Don't get me wrong. My mother was a wonderful parent and a truly special person. Still, I always wondered what my father was like beyond the stories she and other family members told me about him. She always called him 'my hero,' but she would never explain why. Now, suddenly, I had the means to find out for myself."

If Price's time machine actually existed—if it was for real—here was a purpose Miller would have gladly used it for had he had his own device. To finally have the chance to meet and get to know the father who was barely a story to him? What a blessing that would be. Miller didn't believe it was actually possible, but for the first time since they had started their conversation many hours before, the reporter was willing to suspend his disbelief. What if it were possible? Suppose Price wasn't an addled crackpot, but actually had a time machine? What could Miller do with such a device? What would he do if he had the opportunity to actually meet and get to know his own father?

Caught up in this new narrative, Miller had to know. "So, did you do it? Did you get to meet him?"

Before Price could answer, the cab pulled up in front of the restaurant. Price handed the driver a couple of bills. "Keep it," he said, airily.

"Thanks, buddy," said the driver, clearly happy about getting a much larger tip than the short drive had warranted.

As the cab drove off, the professor directed Miller into the restaurant. "Yes, I did get to meet him. And it was one of the most joyous—and painful—days of my life."

FATHER TIME

It was the World of Tomorrow, or at least the World of Tomorrow as seen from 1965. Stereophonic hi-fis. Color television consoles and miniature black-and-white TV sets. Compact and stylish clock radios. There was even technological wizardry that would not have been out of place at the World's Fair, then wrapping up its second year in Flushing Meadows Park. Video cameras for home use. A personal computer that could fit on a desk. Two-way video telephones. Yes, to the people wandering around the vast exhibition hall, the World of Tomorrow was certainly going to be an amazing place.

However, I had come to this consumer showcase in Manhattan with a different agenda in mind. While others were oohing and aahing over these electronic marvels, I was heading over to the display for the Matsushita Electric Corporation of America. There, the assistant marketing director was fiddling with a color television with what the sign on top promised was a massive 24-inch screen.

"Harry, I'm not finding anything in color *on* at the moment."

"Keep looking, Sam. There's got to be something."

Sam was the guy changing channels. That was my father.

He looked a little younger than in the picture my mother kept on the mantle while I was growing up. In the photo, there had been a few touches of gray in his black, close-cropped hair. It must have been taken a few years in the future. The man in front of me now was a young businessman dressed in a navy suit, a white shirt, and dark maroon tie, while the slightly older, portlier, and balding Harry was in the same outfit, only the suit was charcoal gray and the tie was dark blue. The shirt, of course, remained white.

Sam flipped around the dial. "News. *I Love Lucy* rerun. *Popeye* cartoons. Old movie. Wait, I've got it. It's the Mets game."

Harry sighed. "The Mets game. Well, it's better than nothing. At least the field will look really green." Sam was adjusting the controls on the set. "Sam, why doesn't the field look green?"

"It's complicated. It's not easy trying to do everything at once…"

Harry, who was apparently Sam's boss, walked over to him and hissed, "Not in front of the customers, Sam."

"Huh?" It took a moment, but Sam got it. "Oh, right. These controls make adjusting the color a breeze," he replied, a little too loudly.

Harry rolled his eyes, but let Sam continue turning the various dials for color, hue, brightness, and contrast. On screen, a 21-year-old Ron Swoboda, then in his rookie year, was running back to catch an easy fly ball. It almost got away from him, but he caught it, and the side was retired. The camera followed the young player running across the outfield toward the Mets dugout.

"This is Ralph Kiner up in the booth," said the off-screen announcer. "The Mets are trailing five to two as we head into the bottom of the sixth inning. We'll be back after these messages."

The screen shifted to a commercial for some shaving cream which the man onscreen was liberally applying to himself. It seemed to be burning up his face.

"Sam, too much red."

"I'm on it." He tweaked the controls a bit more, and the man's complexion scaled back to a healthier pink flesh tone.

I watched these adjustments from a distance, trying to figure out how I would approach Sam. He had died when I was only three, so I never really knew him. My memories were all second—hand, from my mother and other family members. My mother moved on in life, but she never remarried. As I got old enough to fend for myself, she resumed what apparently had been an active social life, but there was never anyone serious. No one could ever replace her "hero."

I wasn't quite sure how to break the ice. It's not like I could introduce myself to him as his son, especially since I was several years older than him. Fortunately Fate—or perhaps it was Time—lent a hand.

A small group had been watching Sam get the color on the screen just right, or perhaps they were watching the game, but now one of them started talking loudly to the other men around him. "I don't know why anyone would buy one of these cheap Japanese knockoffs. If I'm buying a color TV, I want to be able to rely on American know-how. I want to know that company will be there down the road if something goes wrong and they need to replace any parts." He was carrying brochures from some of the other exhibitors: Admiral, Sylvania, Philco, Motorola. "Why would

I want a TV set from a company with a name I can't even pronounce like Matsoshuster?"

"Actually," said Sam, "Our brand name is Panasonic. And our models feature the latest solid state technology."

The loudmouth was about to answer, but I saw my opening. "That's true. Japanese technology is quickly becoming world class. In fact, in ten years you'll probably not only have a Japanese television set, but drive a Japanese car, as well."

"Oh yeah, and what makes you such an expert?" he sneered, clearly not enjoying being challenged.

I put out my hand. "Wilford Price, professor of physics. And your area of expertise is…?"

"Go ahead, Mitch. Tell him how an insurance salesman knows more about electronics than a physics professor," goaded one of the other men.

"Ah, the hell with it," Mitch said, stalking off. His friends rushed to catch up with him, and I was left standing there alone with Sam.

"Wilford Price? I wonder if we're related." I turned to Sam, and he took my still unshaken hand. "Sam Price. It's not that unusual a name but, still, you never know."

"Small world," I agreed.

We spent the next half hour talking shop. Every so often he'd have to go demonstrate something or hand out brochures featuring the latest items from Panasonic's catalog, but eventually they'd move on, and we'd resume our conversation. I had checked up on the sorts of consumer electronics that were in the pipeline, so that I could sound like I was in the know. Sam was interested in a project Xerox was working on that would allow for the transmission of documents over phone lines, which they would release the following year as the Telecopier. I mentioned that I had heard rumors that Sony was working on a home video recording system, but that was probably some years away. Sam insisted that if any company was going to introduce the home recording of television, it would be Panasonic. I already knew the two companies would eventually go head to head with competing systems a decade from now, with Panasonic backing the VHS system which ultimately prevailed over Sony's Betamax, but I thought it prudent now to just remark on how such technology would transform television viewing. Sam agreed, but complained that the problem was that Americans still thought of Japanese products as nothing but cheap toys and transistor radios.

Along about 5:30, Harry came over. "Quitting time, Sam. Call it a day. I'll see you tomorrow morning bright and early, and in full color."

Sam gave a rueful laugh. "Only one more day of this."

"Be glad we're not required to deal with the public every day." Harry turned to me. "And I appreciate your speaking up earlier. Sam is right. We've got a great line of products, but it is a real uphill battle convincing the public that we're selling quality, not crap."

"It was nothing—"

"And since tomorrow is the last day of the show, I'd like to give you a little thank you."

Sam and I looked at his boss. "It's really not necessary," I started to say, but then accepted the small box he thrust at me. For a moment I was taken aback, as it was roughly the same size as the box my time machine had come in. It couldn't possibly be…

Sam smiled. "You're going to love this. It's an electric pencil sharpener. You'll have all the other professors coming into your office just to sharpen their pencils."

"What can I say?" What could I say? I hadn't used a pencil in years. Between my laptop and my tablet and my smart phone, the last time I recalled physically writing something was when I was asked to sign the department birthday card to Dr. Surkis. "Thank you so much. I've never seen one of these before."

"It's great," said Sam. "You'll find yourself breaking pencil points on purpose, just so you can sharpen them again."

"What an amazing age we live in," I agreed. I wondered what these were selling for on eBay.

We were interrupted by the public address system: "Attention everyone, we'll be closing in fifteen minutes. Please start heading to the exits. Attention. We're closing in fifteen minutes."

"Say, professor, do you have to be somewhere right now? I'd love to hear more about your work," said Sam. "Perhaps you could join us for a drink?"

Harry put up his hands. "I'll have to pass. I've got an hour commute back to Suffern, and that's not counting the half hour it's going to take me just to get out of the garage here. Nice to meet you, professor." With that, he grabbed his attaché case, and turned to join the throngs heading for the exit.

Sam turned to me. "I guess it's just you and me, then, if that's okay."

I put the electric pencil sharpener in the trade show bag filled with advertisements and promotional items. "Sam," I said with a smile, "that would be just fine."

I had done my homework about 1965 electronics, but not about 1965 bars, and that's where I almost tripped myself up. Sam and I sat at the bar at some watering hole not far from the trade show. "What'll it be?" asked the bartender, in the time honored method of his profession.

"I'll take Manhattan," quipped Sam, the double entendre referencing both the song and the drink apparently still having some currency.

"Do you have Laphroaig?" I asked.

"Gesundheit," responded the bartender.

"No, I meant do you have any single malts?"

The bartender looked at me as if I were insane. "This is a bar, buddy. You want a malted, you can go the drugstore on the corner."

"I don't want a malted," I said. "I want a single malt. Do have any top shelf liquor or not?"

"I don't know what you're talking about. We got what you see behind me, and that doesn't include any chocolate malt."

Sam put his arm on my shoulder. "Excuse my friend. He'll take a Chivas, neat." He turned to me, "Do you want water on the side?"

"That would be nice."

"A Chivas, and water on the side." The bartender proceeded to fill the order while Sam took a good look at me. "Single malt, eh? Pretty fancy for a professor. You're not likely to find a neighborhood bar that carries that as a matter of course."

Instead of complaining about the ignorance of the bartender—and the bars of 1965—I realized I had made a mistake. "How do you know so much about scotch?" I asked Sam, hoping to shift attention from my gaffe.

"One of my college buddies spent his junior year in Europe."

"Majoring in distilleries?"

"Well, he spent some time in Scotland. He came back with some fancy preferences and a very well stocked liquor cabinet," said Sam with a laugh. "He claimed that someday we'd all be sharing his high falutin' tastes."

The bartender came with our drinks. He put the Manhattan in front of Sam, complete with a cherry, and put the neat glass of blended scotch in front of me, giving me the fish eye as he provided a goblet of water as well. I would require no more than a drop or two, but apparently no one had ever asked him for this. I took a hollow stirrer from the bin at the edge of the bar and used it to draw a bit of water out of the goblet, then added it to the scotch. I watched the reaction as the amber beverage opened up, but the bartender had already turned his attention to the Bloody Mary someone had ordered, and Sam was savoring his cherry. My *savoir faire* was for naught.

Finally Sam put the now-cherryless stem down on his napkin, raised his glass, and turned to me. I did likewise. "To the future," he toasted. I found it hard to disagree, and we clinked glasses. He put his glass down and turned to me. "So, professor, are you married?"

Ah, we were going to engage in some male bonding. Well, that's what I came here for. "No, I haven't met the right woman yet. What about you?"

"I'm enjoying the bachelor life for the moment, although I'll settle down eventually. But I hear what you're saying. It's all about finding the right woman."

I raised my glass. "To the right woman." Sam's attention, however, was not on my glass, but at a table with two young women sharing a laugh as their colorful drink order arrived. They were conservatively dressed, looking as if they had just come from work.

Sam gave me a nudge. "While we're waiting for Miss Right, I'm willing to settle for Miss Right Now." He raised his glass in their direction. They noticed, and responded by laughing and then making a show of not responding. If I live to be a hundred, I'll never understand human mating rituals, which is probably why I was still single. Sam, however, saw this as the go-ahead. "Let's go make some new friends, professor. I call dibs on the blonde."

He threw a few dollars on the bar to cover our drinks, and then led the way over to their table. "Good evening, ladies," he said, offering a friendly smile. "Are you waiting for someone, or might we join you?"

The blonde looked at her friend, who gave a slight nod, and then turned to us. "Please do. I'm Myrna, and this is Lois. We work at Brentano's." When I looked blank, she added, "It's a bookstore."

"Of course it is. You'll have to excuse the professor. He's in from out of town. I'm Sam, and I'm with Panasonic."

"Is that an airline?" asked Myrna.

"No, it's an electronics company. We make TVs and radios—"

"—and electric pencil sharpeners," I chimed in.

"Yes," said Sam, giving me a look suggesting that I not interfere with his closing the sale. "Professor Price—Bill here—has been advising me on some of his cutting-edge research."

Bill? That was a new one on me. I suppose he figured it sounded better than Wilford.

"That sounds so interesting," said Lois, the brunette. "I was doing inventory in our science department today." I turned to smile at Lois, and got a shock. I was looking at a much younger version of my own mother. "You look familiar," she said to me. "Have you been in our Fifth Avenue store?"

"No, I'm afraid not," I managed to get out. This was beyond awkward. I was playing wingman for my father, although that's not a word he would have used, and it was to help him score with someone *other* than my mother. Which left her to focus her attention on...

"I'm fascinated by science," she said earnestly. "I've been following the Gemini missions. Can you believe that astronaut actually walked in space?"

"No. Yes. I mean, NASA is doing fine work, and is an inspiration to all of us."

Sam gave a nervous laugh. "The professor doesn't get out much, I guess." He and the blonde shared a laugh at my expense, while Lois patted my hand. "I'm sure the work you're doing is very important, too."

Yes, I'm researching the impact that a time machine might have on the Oedipal complex. The situation was spinning out of control fast, and my only reference point besides Freud was *Back to the Future*. I remembered seeing the movie when I was in high school, and the Michael J. Fox character found himself in a similar dilemma. How did he get out of it?

"Tell them about the home recording machines," urged Sam, while trying to call the cocktail waitress over to order another round.

"I've got a reel-to-reel tape recorder," offered Myrna.

Lois turned to me encouragingly. "Is it like that?"

Think, Wilford, think. "Well, the idea is to let people record video the same way they record audio." Myrna looked confused. "The pictures as well as the sound."

She brightened. "You mean I could record my stories on the days I have to work?"

"I don't understand. Your stories?"

"My stories, you know. Like *Search for Tomorrow* and *The Guiding Light*. If you miss more than a few days, it can get very confusing, trying to catch up." Myrna turned to Lois. "Can you imagine that?"

Sam finally caught the eye of the waitress, who came over. "Can I get you another round?"

Myrna looked at her watch. "Six-thirty. No, I'd better not. Dave will be expecting me home."

Now it was Sam's turn to looked confused. "Dave? Who's Dave?"

"My husband. If I leave now, I should be home in Brooklyn in less than an hour." She rose and grabbed her pocketbook. "It's been a pleasure meeting you two. Lois, are you coming?"

Lois gave her friend a funny smile. "No, you go ahead, Myrna. I don't have anyone waiting for me except my cat. I'll see you tomorrow."

Myrna shrugged her shoulders, waved at Sam and me, and left. Now this was supremely awkward. Sam had struck out, and by whatever unwritten rules we were playing by—perhaps the law of the jungle—I apparently had staked a claim on Lois, the woman who in a few years would be giving birth to me. If I managed to survive this without erasing myself from Time all together, there was going to be a whole chapter in my treatise warning time travelers not to visit their parents.

"So, Professor Bill, how long are you in town for?" Mom? Are you flirting with me? Ick!

Sam saw the handwriting on the wall and started to get up. I had to come up with something, and I suddenly realized it wasn't an old movie that I needed. It was a card game or, more exactly, a joke: 52 Card Pickup. I needed to throw caution to the wind. I turned to Lois and roughly grabbed her wrist. I hoped I wasn't leaving a bruise. "Taking off in the morning, babe. Just got time to take you back to my hotel room for a quick fling."

She tried to pull her hand away. "Professor, we've only just met…"

I leered at her. "Don't act all virginal with me. You're hot to trot and I'm raring to go, too. We can order in room service and make it an all-nighter." Lois stood up to try to get away from me, but I held on tight. "Can the shy act, honey, you're not fooling anyone. I just know—"

I never got to finish the sentence. I was suddenly turned around so my face could meet Sam's fist. I was knocked into my seat, and which fell backward onto the floor with a crash. One of the glasses on the table flew off and shattered on impact. "Maybe that's the way they talk to women at your fancy college, but here we treat them with respect." Sam turned to Lois. "I just met this bozo this afternoon. I'm terribly sorry. I didn't know physics professors could be such creeps."

Lois had gathered her things, but now went over to Sam and gave him a chaste peck on the cheek. "My hero."

Offering her his arm, he led her out of the saloon. I heard him say, "Can I make it up to you with dinner?" They were already gone before she responded.

The bartender had come out to prevent any further altercation, but now simply pulled me roughly to my feet. "I think you better go, mister. This is a classy establishment." I put up my hands to indicate surrender. I started gathering my own things when the cocktail waitress came over with a napkin with some ice in it.

"You all right, mister? That was some wallop," she said, handing me the improvised ice pack.

I broke out in a huge smile. "All right? This is the happiest day of my life."

AGED IN THE CASK

"Laphroaig, please," Professor Price said to the waiter.

"Of course. Neat? Or with water?"

"Water on the side, please."

"Very good. And for you, sir?"

Miller shrugged. "Who am I to argue? I'll have the same."

"Very good. Take your time with the menus while I go get your drinks."

While the waiter went off to fill their drink orders, Miller couldn't quite believe the tale Price had just related. "I thought you said it was painful. It was also the happiest day of your life?"

The professor was still smiling. "Indeed it was. It was both. Think about it. I had met my father, gotten a measure of the man, and proved instrumental in setting him up with my mother. How many people can claim to have arranged for their own birth?"

"And don't forget the electric pencil sharpener. Do you still have it, or did you sell it on eBay?"

The waiter came over and set down their drinks. Price made it clear we weren't ready to order dinner yet. "Bring over the artichoke dip. We'll nibble on that while we're making up our minds."

"Very good, sir," the waiter said, as he left to attend to his other tables.

"Lucky I'm a regular here. Now where was I? Yes, I still have that pencil sharpener. Works like a charm." He grinned again.

Miller followed the professor's lead in adding a drop or two of water to the fine scotch. "I'm still not clear why getting slugged by your father made you so happy, other than getting out of an awkward situation."

"To my Dad," toasted Price, and Miller had no choice but to clink glasses and take a sip.

"Well, Willy, what's the rest of the story?"

"The rest of the story? I never saw my father again. I knew I had pressed my luck, but now I had some good memories. And there's something more. I think he knew."

"Knew what? That you were from the future?"

"No, I can't say that for certain. I'm a scientist. I look at the evidence."

Miller couldn't resist the dig. "And I'm a reporter. I haven't seen any evidence yet."

Price sighed. "In good time, in good time. But consider what happened with my father. First, when he punched me, it was more of a stage punch. He really only pushed me back into the chair which fell over. I think he knew that I was trying to help him out, and that I was opening the door for him to 'rescue' my mother." Miller raised a skeptical eyebrow. "And then there's the matter of my name."

"Your name?"

"Come on, Max, use that analytical reporter's brain. Sam knew my name was Wilford. If he had thought I was some masher who was going to attack the woman he eventually married, he could hardly pick that name for his son. I think it was his way of saying thank you."

"But wait, didn't your mother hear your name as well? She couldn't know you were faking it."

"I had been introduced as Professor Bill. She never heard the name 'Wilford.' I once asked her where it came from, and she said it was an old family name from my father's side."

The two sat quietly for a moment, sipping from their respective glasses. The heavy curtains around the room muffled sound so that voices didn't really carry. In the silence, Miller heard murmurs, but nothing distinct. Finally, he broke the silence. "Okay, Willy. I can't get upset with you. It's not like I'm not getting paid for today, and you're treating me to a lovely dinner, and you're a fabulous storyteller. In fact, I have a friend who is involved with a proposed revival of *The Twilight Zone*, and I'm going to recommend you to him. I think you may have missed your calling."

Price smiled. "The story is far from over."

The waiter came over with their artichoke dip appetizer and withdrew. Clearly he understood that the two men were in no hurry and had much to discuss. Having served Price before, he knew he would be well taken care of by the end of the evening.

Miller watched as the professor scooped up some of the dip with a piece of pita bread. "Fine. Let's assume I believe everything you've told me, and review the story so far. You've gotten a time machine from yourself."

"My future self." He took a bite. "You really must try this."

Miller rolled his eyes. "Of course," he said, dunking the pita in the dip. "So what have you learned from using this machine? You tried to change *your* past, and you failed. You tried to change major events in history, and you failed. You tried to learn about the future, and other than some sports betting tips, you failed. You met your father and engaged in a barroom brawl that led to him meeting your mother. From where I stand, it seems to me that if you had never gotten this machine in the first place, absolutely nothing would have changed. So all your journeys lead to the same dead end. There really isn't any story for me here."

"Max, Max, Max," Price said indulgently, "You forgot that I prevented a nuclear war between the United States and Canada."

The reporter raised his hands in surrender. "Oh yes, of course. How could I have forgotten? The clincher for your story is that you actually did have an impact. You prevented a war that no one on Earth can remember happening."

"That's because I prevented it."

Miller rubbed his eyes. "Willy, I know that you're not a journalist, but how do I sell this story to my editor? Not only is there no evidence for anything you've told me, but the bottom line is that, as far as anyone can tell, things would be exactly the same whether or not your time machine is real." With that, Miller drained his glass. "So, assuming for the moment that everything you've said is true, what did you do next? Having hit one road block after another, where did you turn?"

Price was beaming. "That's the first question you got right."

"Ouch," said Miller, as he put down his now empty glass.

"No, no, don't misunderstand me. I'm not criticizing your profession-alism, Max. You're doing your job. Believe me, I get that."

"So why was that question different?"

The professor offered his paternal smile again. "Because it was the first question you've asked that I had asked myself. I had been treating the time machine like someone with a new laptop who couldn't be bothered to read the instructions. I saw how it operated and used it, but I really had learned very little at all." With that, Price raised his hand, summoning the waiter over. "There's much more to tell, but we ought to get dinner. They indulge me here, but they don't stay open all night."

The waiter arrived with his pad and pen ready to take down their orders. Price looked at Miller. "Please, whatever you'd like."

Miller smiled. "Since I'm not picking up the tab and have put in a more-than-full day, I'll have the prime rib au jus, medium rare. And a baked potato."

"Excellent," said the waiter. "And the professor?"

"Ah, I love red meat. Unfortunately, red meat does not love me. I do hope you'll spare me a bite. I think I can handle a taste." He turned to the attentive water. "I'll have the grilled swordfish and rice pilaf. And an order of asparagus on the side, lightly broiled in olive oil. We'll share."

"You do know your way around the menu," said Miller admiringly, as the waiter departed.

"I don't cook much, so I've been here often," said Price. "I do hope you like asparagus."

"As long as it's not mixed with broccoli," said the reporter, wrinkling his nose.

The professor laughed. "No, the asparagus here is entirely broccoli free. Now, where was I?"

"You had a time machine and had learned nothing."

Price sighed. "Well, not *nothing*, but as you may have gathered, I'm much more interested in applied science than in theoretical physics. I am my father's son in many ways. He went into sales and I went into research, but we were both interested in how things worked and coming up with new things. I was happy to leave the deep dish thinking—the 'why'—to others."

The young reporter, who had probably not been so anesthetized since his college days, was feeling no pain. He relaxed in his chair, not even bothering to take notes. "So what did you do next?"

The professor took on a serious expression. "I decided that I had been going about this all wrong. I had been dashing hither and yon as if that's what time travel was all about. I realized that I needed to understand the theoretical underpinnings of the device as well as explore exactly what it was doing to time. My future self had yet to fully understand how it worked, particularly how Time decided what could or could not be changed. Having defined the problem, it seemed to me that now was the time to do the hard work."

Miller saw that Price was getting ready to launch into another long tale. For all the drinking he had been doing—and for all the drinking reporters were traditionally supposed to be able to do—he thought he could handle one more, particularly with a juicy plate of roast beef yet to come. He gestured to the waiter to bring him another. The waiter turned to Price, who silently indicated he had had enough. Miller might pay for this indulgence in the morning, but he didn't care. He had earned it.

"So where did your next adventure take you?" asked Miller.

"Why, the library, of course. It was time to actually do some research. I was a bit concerned as I entered the building, but I was in my own time, and no one stopped me or even looked twice. I went over to the office where I would be interrogated some decades from now, but it was locked. I decided that this indicated that I had a free hand and no one would try and stop me. I began my research into what theoretical physicists had said about time travel."

The waiter placed a fresh glass of scotch in front of Miller and withdrew the empty. "Okay, Willy. You went to the library. What did you find?"

"Not much," admitted the professor. "It's not like this was a major area of research. I was almost ready to give up when I stumbled across an article by Professor Henry Gondelman. It was a review of some then-new book, but in recapitulating the research on subatomic particles, it was apparent he knew much more than he was letting on. He suggested that new work into neutrinos might cause us to reconsider how Einstein had taught us to think about the universe, but it was all hints and implications. It was as if he knew more than he was saying. So I started researching Professor Gondelman."

Miller took this in the same way he had taken everything else Price had offered. It made no sense whatsoever. There was no question, though, that Price was entertaining. Who knew where this new yarn would lead? He reminded himself that, in exchange for all the hospitality he had been receiving from the academic, he was now required to play the straight man. "Okay, I'll bite. And when you researched Professor Gondelberg, what did you discover?"

"Gondelman," he corrected. "I read several of his articles, and then I found his book that described the theoretical underpinnings for time travel. He argued that there was still much work to be done, but that he believed that it was, in fact, possible."

"Okay," said Miller. "You found the book. Did it provide any useful clues? Did it actually lead to anything?"

"Oh my, yes," said the professor, who became visibly more animated. "Absolutely. What was amazing was not his idea that time travel was theoretical possible. That wasn't news to me. I already knew it was real. No, what was amazing was even more startling."

Across the table, the reporter sighed. "You're going to make me ask, aren't you? Okay, Willy, what was the most startling thing about the book?"

Price reached into the briefcase he had placed on the empty seat next to him and pulled out a copy of the book. "This isn't the library's copy. I tracked down a copy and purchased it on my own. You'll see why I needed it. Read what it says here." He opened the book to a page near the very beginning, and handed it to the reporter, pointing to what he should read.

"And I'd like to thank Dr. Wilford Price, whose insights and assistance proved to be invaluable. I could not have done this without him," Miller read. He looked up. "That's very nice. I know how nasty academic infighting can be with people trying to hog credit."

Price smiled again. "You're missing the point. Look at the copyright page."

The reporter flipped back a few pages. It took him a moment to realize the significance of what he was seeing. Then he looked at the professor with a look that was something new. "1972? Is that a misprint?"

"No, it's quite real. I have copies of the few reviews the book received in the scientific press."

"But how is that possible?"

"Ah, that's the second good question you've asked since we've sat down. Laphroaig obviously agrees with you. Before you ask how it's possible, I think you already know why it's an excellent question. This book came out two years after I was born."

DEPARTMENT MEETING

My first surprise came when I saw that Henry Gondelman's office in 1972 was where it was. It was my office. Of course I wouldn't arrive to teach here for another couple of decades, and I didn't think my two-year-old self would have much use for it. I knocked on the door.

"You're using the door now? Come in already," shouted an annoyed voice from within. I entered and received my second surprise. Before I even had a chance to take in the similarities and differences in his use of the space, I was startled by his greeting. "It's about time you got here."

"Professor Gondelman?"

"Yes, yes, I'm Henry Gondelman. Get on with it."

He was sitting at my desk—er, his desk—tamping some tobacco into a pipe. The tiny photograph on the dust jacket hadn't done him justice. His decidedly unstylish black framed glasses suited him, contrasting with the shock of white hair that topped his head. I closed the door behind me as much for privacy as to get my bearings. I was feeling a sense of *déjà vu*, being in what was my own office yet not my office, and his reaction to my arrival made it all that much stranger. I finally found my voice.

"Professor Gondelman, were you expecting me?"

He lit a match and took a puff of his pipe, and then focused his attention on me. "You're Wilford Price. You teach physics here at the turn of the century. This will be your office. You have a time machine and you want to give it to me. Let's get it over with. I have work to do."

Now I was completely confused. "Professor Gondelman..."

"We'll save some time if you just call me Henry. Not that saving time seems to be your long suit."

"Professor Gondel... okay, Henry. How do you know who I am, and that I have a time machine?"

Gondelman took another puff of his pipe and placed it in the ashtray that would be *verboten* in the office in my time. He took off his glasses and wiped them with his pocket handkerchief. Both glasses and handkerchief were returned to their proper places. "How do I know?

Because this is the fourth time you've shown up in my office in the last half hour."

This was getting more and more baffling. I was beginning to feel a bit unsteady. "Would you mind if I took a seat?"

He waved toward a chair near his desk as he picked up his pipe and relit it. "Be my guest. It's not like you're staying very long."

I sat down and took a deep breath. Something was going on, and while I didn't fully understand it, I began to realize that neither did he. The problem is that we had different pieces of the puzzle. "I think we both need to explain ourselves. You see, up until this moment, I've never come back to see you."

This got Gondelman's attention. It didn't take him long to work through the problem in his head. "There's no touch of gray in your hair. Your face is unlined. You must be twenty or thirty years younger." He snapped his fingers. "Of course. You just got the machine, didn't you? You discovered my research and came back to see me."

"Yes," I said, excitedly. "It's an honor to meet you...."

"Fine, fine, from what I've been led to believe, it's an honor to meet you, too. Let's put aside the Amy Vanderbilt manners and get on with it. Let me tell you what my day has been like, and we can proceed from there." I nodded in agreement. He took a puff of his pipe, and continued. "A half hour ago you first arrived. Obviously, as I now understand, it was a future you. You said you had hit a number of dead ends in your temporal research, even with my help. Of course I had no idea what this person, who I presumed to be a madman, was talking about. I had never seen him before, and he was talking like we had done much work together. I was trying to figure out how to call for help without alarming him when he attempted to give me a package."

"A package?"

"He said it was a duplicate time machine. He—or you—claimed that it would be a lot easier if I starting moving around in time right away. He stepped forward, and I prepared to defend myself as best I could, when suddenly he disappeared. Thus, when you showed up, I thought it was him again. Well, it was him, but it was an earlier him, which is to say, you."

"I've only been doing this for a short while," I replied. "Please finish your story, and then I'll tell you mine. Don't worry about confusion along the timeline. I'll ask if I don't understand something. I suspect it's going to get more confusing before we're through."

Gondelman took another puff, and favored me with his first smile since I had arrived. "You have no idea. You came two more times before *you* finally arrived."

"Did I say or do anything on those other visits? How far apart were they spaced?"

The old professor laughed. "My immediate reaction was that one of my graduate students must have mixed something into my tobacco and that I had hallucinated the whole thing. Then you reappeared. You seem annoyed."

I had no doubt that some future version of myself was responsible for this, but I still didn't get what was motivating me. "What did I say?"

"You said that Time didn't want me to have the time machine. You claimed that one could change some things in the past, but not others, and you had hoped short circuiting the process where I became fully engaged in the project might solve the problems he had been grappling with for so long."

"Really? Did I explain what I meant? Did you understand me?"

"I didn't have a clue. I still don't. I'm hoping you'll be able to explain that to me. In any case, he said since he couldn't just hand me the time machine, perhaps he could just put it down on my desk and then back away before returning to his own time."

I began to see what the problem was. "Time has a way of preventing those changes that are not permitted." I told him about my experience with the spilled coffee.

He pulled out a notebook. "Do you mind if I take notes?"

I nodded my approval, and gave him a brief recap of my adventures into the past. When I finished, he said, "Interesting. So you can come back and have this conversation with me, but your future self's attempt to transfer the technology to me apparently would be too disruptive."

"That's my theory. On the other hand, some future version of myself gave *me* the machine. It sounds like he—or I—believed you should have the machine, but he wasn't allowed to hand it over to you. So what happened when I tried to put it on your desk?"

Gondelman pointed to a space on his desk that was empty. "You put it down there and took two steps back. Then the package started to spark, and it and you vanished. Five minutes later, you were back again."

I couldn't imagine what my future self was going through. "Are you under the impression that these visits were sequential? That you experienced them in the same order as my future self did?"

He took a puff on the pipe and then reached for his matches to relight it. "That's a good question," he said after he relit the bowl. "Yes, I do believe that this was a series of attempts one after another where he—you —spaced them out so you didn't have several versions of yourself bumping into each other at the same time."

"What happened the third time?"

"This time there was no package. This time you tried to hand me a large manila envelope. You barely choked out the words, 'The schematic designs…' before vanishing yet again. So when you showed up— meaning you personally—I naturally assumed it was going to be yet another attempt by this future you."

We sat there in silence for a moment, Gondelman puffed on his pipe while I tried to digest all this new information. "Do you have any idea when my future self came from?"

He gave me a good, long look. "When do *you* come from? I'd guess he was maybe thirty years or so older than you are now."

"I'm from 1997," I said. "I'm 27 years old." Gondelman raised his eyebrows. "I was something of a prodigy. I finished college at 17, and had my Ph.D. at 21."

He favored me with another smile. "Ah, a fellow prodigy. That would explain a lot. In any case, the version of you who preceded your own arrival looked more like he was in his late fifties." Gondelman put down his pipe. "All right. I've told you my story, and you've told me yours. Why don't you tell me what *you're* doing here."

I pulled my copy of his book out of my bag. "Henry, this is where our story really begins." I handed the volume over to him, hesitating for just a moment. Would he be allowed to touch it? Would I disappear? Nothing of the sort happened, and Gondelman spent a long moment looking at the cover with a smile. Then he turned it over.

"Oh no." What had happened? Was Time about to unleash its fury at us?

"What's the matter?"

"I always hated that picture of me. If it's really possible to make at least some changes in the time line, I'm going to try to get a better photo on the dust jacket."

"Your book comes out later this year. Have you finished writing it?"

He looked up. "Almost done, almost done. I'm struggling with the last chapter, the one where I try to make the case that we have to consider that movement in time is at least theoretically possible." His face suddenly broadened into a grin. "You know, I can just copy the chapter out of your book. It's not really plagiarism if you steal it from yourself, is it?" He returned his attention to the book and opened it. Or, at least, he tried to. The pages seemed stuck together.

"See, this is what's maddening," I said. "You're allowed to see your future book, but you're not allowed to read it. My future self could give me the time machine, but couldn't give it to you."

"You think it has something to do with me?" Gondelman seemed perturbed by the idea.

"No, not you personally. It seems there are rules governing the transmission of, well, *anything* through time. My future self said he had been working on the problem for years, but was unable to derive the rules that would allow him to know what was and wasn't permitted. All he knew was that the rules were there."

Gondelman handed the book back to me. It opened easily. "Hmm, you know, I could try to read you the chapter…"

The professor put up his hands. "No, no, no. We may not understand the rules, but we have to respect them. Clearly, what is required is that I actually work through my theories and not take any short cuts. Still, I have to ask if you have read it. Did my conclusions make sense to you?"

I slipped the book back into my briefcase. "Frankly, no," I started, and he seemed disappointed. "Don't get me wrong. I'm not saying you're mistaken. I'm saying I couldn't follow all of your reasoning. That's why I've come back to work with you. I want to understand it myself. You're a theoretician. I'm more at home in applied physics."

He reached for his pipe and tobacco pouch. "Ah yes, the great divide in physics. It's like the nature versus nurture arguments the biologists and psychologists have."

"I wonder what they argue about in the chemistry department," I wondered.

"Probably who has to pick up the check, if they're anything like the professors I know. If it doesn't smell or blow up, they seem more interested in mixing drinks than chemicals." When I laughed, he added, "It's good to see that some things haven't changed." We enjoyed the moment of faculty one-upsmanship and then, suddenly, he was all business.

"So, without telling me the details, what is it that baffles you about this chapter of mine on time?"

"Well, I suppose we can start with your calculations in which you transmute time into just another spatial coordinate without explaining how the transference of mass doesn't cause an explosion on one end or an implosion on the other."

Relighting his pipe, he leaned back in his swivel chair. "Yes, that's been bothering me a lot, too. Thank goodness for computers. When I started in this game I had to do calculations on a slide rule." He paused. "You young pup, do you even know what a slide rule is?"

I looked him right in the eye. He might be the expert here, but I was no grad student. "I most certainly do. I saw one in a museum."

"Ouch," Gondelman replied. "Okay, I deserved that. Let me show you my latest calculations, and perhaps we can figure it out together." I got out of my chair and started looking around the room. "What is it? I assume the men's room is in the same place in your time if you need it."

"I was looking for your computer."

"*My* computer? The university's mainframe is across campus. It would hardly fit in my office." He rose and walked across the room to where there was some shelving. Back in 1997, that's where I would keep my extra boxes of floppies. I didn't know what to make of what he was carrying. He came back to his desk holding what seemed to be two huge, bound stacks of paper. "Do you actually have your own computer? How can they afford it? Is your chair endowed?"

"Henry, I have a laptop." His puzzled expression indicated I had to explain. "It's a portable, personal computer." I couldn't imagine a world where there was one computer for the entire campus, and everyone had to wait in line for their turn.

Gondelman took it all in stride. He smiled. "Ah, the future must be a wonderful place. Do you have flying cars and jet packs as well?"

"No, we're still working on that."

He must have read the expression on my face. I was a lousy poker player. "I can see you're pulling my leg. Well, this isn't exactly the Stone Age. We landed a man on the moon and I have a color television at home. I may have to wait my turn to run my material through the computer—I don't like to pull rank and jump the line—but I do have a pocket calculator." He pulled something out of his pocket. "You ever see this?

It's the Bowmar Brain. Got it at a steal for under $200." I didn't have the heart to tell him that by the time I entered middle school, a few years from now, they'd be giving these away as prizes in cereal boxes.

"Very nice," I said instead. "So, what's with all the paper? Do you need some help with that?"

"These are my printouts. How else are we going to go over the calculations?" With that, he opened the cover, and I saw hundreds of pages of type printed out on green-and-white striped paper. It might not be the Stone Age, exactly, but suddenly I felt very out of my time.

Several hours later, Gondelman had walked me through his work to date. He might be treating me like a colleague—even an advanced colleague—but my head hadn't hurt this much since my grad school days. Both of us had notepads full of calculations and comments. There was stuff I had written down that I wouldn't even have understood when I first woke up that morning. "So it's the displacement caused by the shift of the mass in time that's the issue."

"Indeed. If you can come back next week, I should have the printout of my latest work, and then we can review that."

The late afternoon sun was coming in through the window, and my stomach was rumbling because I hadn't eaten all day. I may have been in 1972 for only a few hours, but according to my internal 1997 clock, I'd already been up for nearly twenty-four hours, and the last thing I'd had to eat was a few pretzels when I had a drink with my father. "You know, Henry, I can't give you the answer out of your book, but I could run your latest calculations through *my* computer in 1997 and be back here in a few minutes."

Gondelman considered that for a moment, and then shook his head. "No, I don't think so."

"Why not? It would save us time."

"Ah, that's exactly the point. I don't want to save time. I want Time to save me."

We had joked about the difference between those working in theoretical and applied physics, but there was a deep truth hidden beneath the gibes. The theoreticians sometimes seemed closer to poets than scientists, which meant they made no sense to practical physicists like me. "I'm afraid I don't follow. Computers in my era are faster and capable of much more than you can do now, and we don't even need punch cards. And no matter how long it takes me, I can be back here seconds after I left."

"You misunderstand, Willy, I'm perfectly all right with you taking your notes with you and bringing the results back. Having to wait for them to key in my data and hoping they get it right the first time is maddeningly slow. What I don't want you to do is come right back. I want to wait. And I'm suggesting you wait on your end as well." He saw my puzzled expression and held up his hand. "I haven't been a very good host. Do you like whiskey?" I smiled. until he opened the bottom drawer of his desk—another example of how things hadn't changed—and pulled out a bottle of Canadian Club. I could see that I would have to research what single malts were available in the United States in 1972.

"I don't know if I should be drinking on an empty stomach."

"Or course not. Give me a moment." He left the office. My mind was reeling. I had just spent several hours with one of the greatest minds in the history of physics, who had come up with the underpinnings for the device that apparently I would be inventing at some future point in history. In a way, I was assisting in my own birth again. I looked up as Gondelman returned with a platter with vegetables, cheese, dip, and crackers. "It's the remnants of the Friday afternoon department wine and cheese hour. Each week, students and faculty let the barriers between them come tumbling down for a brief social hour. The department chairman seems to think that it makes the professors appear more like human beings and less like gods."

"Department chairs," I smiled in agreement. "Some things haven't changed at all."

Gondelman pushed aside the papers on his desk and set down the platter. I helped myself to some sliced peppers and onion dip while he poured a bit of the Canadian whiskey into the two tumblers he also kept in the bottom drawer. I wonder if those who wrote about the history of science realized the crucial role alcohol had played in the march of progress. Probably not. People still believed that Newton discovered gravity from an apple dropping on his head, instead of him falling on his ass after a night out with the boys. Gondelman raised his glass, "To Time!"

I could only clink glasses and echo the sentiment. "To Time." We sipped the blended whiskey, and I looked forward to the bottle of Macallan I had at home.

"That's much better," he said.

I returned his smile. It had been a productive day, and I knew I would sleep well tonight. Or twenty-five years from now. Whatever. "So why don't you want me to come back right away with the results?"

"Willy, this is where experience trumps ambition. You've got a brilliant mind. We have very different approaches, but I appreciate what you bring to the equation. I don't know if I could have gotten as far as we have today without your help. I intend to acknowledge your assistance in my book."

I said nothing. I didn't want to break the mood and, besides, I didn't know if I'd be allowed to tell him that I already knew that he would. "Thank you," was all I said.

"Let's assume you go home and go to sleep. I see how tired you are. You wake up the next day and, using your lap computer, you get the answers in seconds that would take me days. Then you return five minutes from now, fully rested and ready to go. Are you starting to see what the problem is?"

"I could come back in the morning."

"Yes, you could. Since you can move about in time you can come back whenever you'd like. I'm going to ask you to wait until Monday."

"It's all the same to me, but why?"

"Willy, we both use computers although I don't think either of us really understands the one that the other is using, but that's entirely beside the point. The most important computer we have is the one up here." He tapped the side of his forehead. "I don't just need to see points plotted along a four axis graph. I need time to process it up here. I need a few days to think about what we've done today and see what new connections I can come up with on my own. Computers are basically bigger versions of this," he said, pulling out his Bowmar Brain. "But real thought, innovation, new connections, only comes from the human brain. Take all the time you need to digest what we've learned today. Days, weeks, even months. Then come back Monday morning at 10 A.M. I've arranged my schedule this semester so that all my classes are on Tuesday, Wednesday, and Thursday. We'll have the whole day free to work. That will also give me the weekend to relax and muse. I do some of my best thinking soaking in the bathtub."

I got what he was saying. It wasn't just about crunching numbers. It was about understanding them. It was about seeing the unexpected connections. I raised my glass. "To hot baths and deep thought."

As it happened it would be several days before I went back. Working out the data hadn't taken long. I had woken up late in the morning and spent a couple of hours playing with it on my laptop. Henry was right. It wasn't enough to know the answer. It was the process that mattered, and I needed time to fully understand the implications of what we had discovered.

Here was the problem: any sort of movement at all required the moving object to displace what was already there. While this wasn't an issue in a perfect vacuum, it was in the world most of us inhabited. If I walked from here to there the oxygen atoms—the "air" consisting of oxygen and numerous other elements present in large or minute quantities —already there would be displaced. When I moved in three dimensional space that was easy enough. They would slide around me or otherwise move as I entered the new space. However when I travelled in time, I was displacing atoms already filling up that space. Worse, I was leaving an emptiness behind me that would have to be filled.

This came to me in, of all places, the bath. I had taken Henry's advice, and took a long soak in the tub, not something I ordinarily did. As I slipped into the water, I realized this was precisely what I had been doing with my time travelling. Adding or removing a bit of water from the tub wouldn't make much of a difference. However, as I lowered myself into the hot water, I saw that the level rose dangerously close to the lip of the tub as I displaced the water with my body.

It got even more complicated. Henry believed that whatever air got displaced in one time was sent to the other time to replace the person or object that had travelled. However, it wasn't enough to replace the volume. One had to replace the mass. You know the old riddle about which weighs more, a pound of feathers or a pound of lead? The answer is they weigh precisely the same, but that the volume of space they take up is different. A pound of lead is a relatively small cube while a pound of feathers amounts to a pretty hefty sack. In other words, it takes up more space. By Henry's calculations, a person who weighed 170 pounds who travelled from 1997 to 1972 (which is to say, me), would need to send back 170 pounds of air, and not merely fill a space that was an inch or two shy of six feet high and 18 inches wide.

This turned out not to be much of a problem in theory (Henry's field) but could be a major issue in practice (mine). So long as time travel was limited to individuals who travelled at different times and to different places, things should balance out. However, if everyone in Manhattan suddenly decided to go back twenty years into the past simultaneously, it could get ugly. That's what I had been calculating. While moving air back and forth in time didn't turn out to be a particular problem, especially since it would be balanced on the return trip, there was a limitation to it. Even putting aside the issue of, say, reintroducing the Black Death from the 14th century to the late 20th, there was the sheer size of the mass being displaced. Suddenly the need for a time patrol—and putting limits on when people could go quite beyond those unknowable rules of Time— made a lot of sense. If all the air rushed out of a city to compensate for the arrival of millions of people simultaneously, it would be disastrous on both ends.

How to cope with this practical limitation on time travel would require some thought. Knowing I had an appointment at a set time with the professor, I gave myself some time in 1997 to mull it over. After almost a week, I had taken it as far as I could, and realized it was time to work with Henry again.

I got out the time travel device and my notebook. I suspected that even with a full battery, my laptop wouldn't do me much good in 1972. I did check to see what single malts might be available in America then, and saw that with a little work, one could find Glenfiddich and Glenlivet. So I changed the coordinates on my device so that I would first arrive at the most well-stocked liquor store in the city, and got a bottle of Glenlivet. I could have taken a cab to the campus, but instead I changed back the spatial coordinates and went a few minutes into the future, arriving just outside Henry's building at 9:15 on Monday morning. I looked around to see if anyone had noticed, but no one had. I headed up to my office— Henry's office—and he was already there.

"Coffee and donuts," he said by way of greeting. "I didn't know how you take it, so I have cream and sugar."

He did indeed, plus a box of a dozen assorted donuts. I might not like them all, but on the other hand, we weren't likely to eat six donuts apiece. At least, I wasn't. "Henry, you are a very gracious host."

"My mother would be proud."

I reached into my briefcase and pulled out the printouts from my analysis. The graphics were impressive, and the several pages of back-up data covered the material well. It took up a lot less paper than his 1972 mainframe computer would have done. "I think this covers the problem."

He skimmed through the pages. "I'll want to study this in detail, but it seems to confirm what I realized when I slipped into my bath Friday night and—"

"—and you saw how the water was displaced. I had the same reaction."

Gondelman smiled. "Great minds do think alike."

We sipped our coffee and I nibbled on a chocolate frosted donut. "So where do we go from here?"

"From here? We finish our coffee and donuts, and then I go and write. We did all the hard work on Friday. I think we're both at the same place now, and these numbers just confirm it," he said, waving the pages.

We both sat down. "But I have so much more to ask."

"As do I, but we have to play out the hand. I know what I have to do to finish the chapter and submit my manuscript. That's obviously the priority. Once that's done, there'll be plenty of time."

I could see the logic in that. "I've just begun to understand the process that lets the machine work."

"Yes, clearly that's your mission in life. It's probably why you were allowed to receive it from your future self, while I couldn't." He looked a bit wistful. "Do you think I could see it?"

I popped the last piece of donut into my mouth and put the Styrofoam cup down on his desk. "I don't know if that's up to me, but we can try. But before I do, if something should happen that causes me to bounce back to 1997, when should I return?"

He took a sip from his own cup. "Let's make it the same time next Monday. I should be able to finish the manuscript by the weekend and get it off to the publisher."

I took the device out of my briefcase and held it in my lap, making no attempt to hand it over to him. He remained seated where he was, but peered intently. I pointed to the different parts. "This is the on/off switch, pretty basic. This is where I set the date and time coordinates." I turned it around. "And this is where I can set the spatial coordinates. If I leave them alone, I simply travel along the T axis and it automatically compensates for the movement of the Earth."

"Fascinating." He moved his seat a little closer, clearly trying not to tempt fate… or Time. "Can you open it?"

I undid a latch on the top. "I haven't completely reverse engineered it, but I did take a look inside. Let's see if you can do the same."

Gondelman spent several moments peering within. "I wouldn't have thought of the design, but I don't see any material in there that's unfamiliar. What's that black box on the right?"

I looked down. "That's the GPS."

"The Gupps?"

"The Global Positioning System device. It seems to be the one part of it that works through time, because the government won't even start work on the project until next year, and it didn't become fully operational until just a few years ago in my time. It's a program that allows you to coordinate yourself anywhere on Earth by connecting with signals from a system of satellites in orbit. They're just starting to integrate GPS with our cell phones."

"What a cell phone? Is it a means of keeping track of prisoners?"

I laughed and pulled out my cell. "No, no, it's a portable telephone. They say some day this will evolve into a device that will include the ability to communicate, conduct financial transactions, and do advanced computing. I don't know if I'll live to see that, but the changes are coming so fast one never knows."

"May I see it?" I handed him the phone, knowing it was worthless in 1972, with no network to connect to. He turned it over in his hand, examining it. "Incredible. I wonder if you would be able to give me the time machine…"

"Henry, I don't think that's a good idea…"

He reached over for the device and there was a flash. I was alone in my office. I knew it was my office because the coffee and donuts were gone and the laptop was sitting on my desk. Clearly, there was a limit to his curiosity although, annoyingly, it didn't seem to include my cell phone, which had remained in 1972 with him. Well, we had planned for this. I set the time machine for a week later, and went back to retrieve it. The phone was there. Gondelman was not.

Could I have misunderstood him? I picked up the phone. The battery was dead, not that it would have worked now anyway. That's when I noticed the envelope with my name on it that had been sitting underneath it. I picked it up, not quite sure if I wanted to open it. Something wasn't right, and I knew that examining what was inside the envelope was going to be a turning point that I might not like.

Inside were two pages. The first page was a letter from Gondelman addressed to me.

> *Dear Willy* (it read),
>
> *Let me start by saying what a real pleasure it was getting to know you and working with you. I want to apologize for what I've done, and I can only hope you'll forgive me and understand. Although we have our different approaches to temporal mechanics, I mean it as no idle flattery when I say that your work equals and possibly surpasses mine. I could not have completed my book without your assistance and collaboration, and have so noted it in my acknowledgements. When the history of temporal mechanics is written—if terms like "history" even have meaning any longer—your name will shine brightly.*
>
> *I finished my manuscript over the weekend before we last met, and it's already off to the publisher. When I was done, I realized that the next logical step in my work had to be actually using a time travel device and exploring its effects. Your future self tried to speed up the process too soon. You/he couldn't hand me the device, but there was nothing stopping me from building one myself. When you showed it to me last Monday, I saw what the missing puzzle piece was: it was literally a black box, the GPS.*
>
> *I built a crude time travel device and jury-rigged your phone to it so that I could travel far enough into the future to obtain a more sophisticated version of it to install. I return your phone intact, if in need of a recharge. I know you're in my office now, because I was standing across the quad in the doorway of the humanities building, and saw you arrive and enter. I then went back to drop off this letter, after going back in time to yesterday in order to type it up.*
>
> *I've spent many years exploring the idea of time travel in theory, and you can hardly blame me for wanting to explore it for real once you showed me it was possible. At least, I hope you won't blame me. I have much to learn and discover, as do you. Now our paths must diverge. I hope we will meet again somewhen.*
>
> *With deep respect and affection,*
> *Henry Gondelman*

I read it twice before I could fully catch my breath. If the letter left me with a mixture of admiration and annoyance, it was the second page that made me glad there was a chair to collapse onto. It, too, was from Henry.

Dear Willy,

I've been traveling through time for more than a decade now, at least in terms of subjective time. In terms of the timeframe I've travelled along, it literally spans eons. I understand so much more now, and—perhaps you'll be pleased to note—what I've discovered has been building on your own research. Talk about paradoxes. Apparently, our breakthroughs have come from standing on each other's shoulders. I now know the answer to the riddle as to which came first, the chicken or the egg? The correct answer is, "Yes."

One of the things I've learned is that there are reasons to close off parts of the timeline to some or all travelers. In fact, using your research, I helped the temporal authorities develop the means to do so. It's why your trips to your future were circumscribed. It's also why you are not going to be able to do what will be your first instinct after leaving here. The week from the time you left last Monday to the time you arrived today is entirely closed to you. You can try, but you will not be able to penetrate the barrier surrounding that time.

I'll be popping into that brief window between my past self dropping off the phone and the first letter and your arrival right now to insert this letter in the envelope as well. Why? I can't really tell you. You need to make these discoveries on your own, just as I needed to build the device on my own. I do know something about the adventure you have ahead, and can tell you this: trust your instincts. Don't go trying to find me. We'll meet again when Time permits.

Let me add one more thing. You have my blessings. I consider you the son I never had.

Until that Time when we meet again, I remain,
Yours, affectionately,
Henry

P.S. Stay away from the stock market. If you want to find a sure bet, find odds makers who will take your bet that someone name Barack Obama will become president in 2008. Apparently, he's a law professor who gets elected to the Illinois legislature in your time. Trust me on this.

DINNER IS SERVED

"**H**e told you to bet on Obama?" Price looked at the reporter. "That's what you got out of that?"

Miller looked chagrined. "Well, that's a lot to swallow. But after listening to this saga of arcane scientific theories and academic betrayal, I have to say that that's a rather prosaic note to end on."

"Can you imagine how frustrated I was? I thought I had found a collaborator, but instead he took off. I went back to 1997 and started reading the news reports. Gondelman vanished off the face of the Earth. His book—considered his crowning achievement—was published later that year in what most people took as a posthumous edition."

"Did you try to go back to find him?"

Price picked at the remains of his salad. "I made an attempt or two, but going back earlier made no sense, and later he was, indeed, gone. As he had promised, the week where I might have pinned him down for an explanation was closed to me."

"What happened when you tried?"

"Nothing. The device simply wouldn't accept those coordinates as valid ones. So it was back to the library. That's where I discovered that his legacy had been preserved by his daughter, Alison. She had finished her graduate work in and took an appointment in the department in 1976. She was already gone by the time I arrived in the mid-1990s, but other than teaching some introductory classes, her chief responsibility seemed to be sifting through her father's papers and organizing them in a way that would be useful to future researchers."

The waiter approached the table with their entrees. A busboy swiftly cleared the table of the remains of appetizers and salads and set down the prime rib in front of Miller and the swordfish in front of Price, with the steaming plate of asparagus placed deftly between them. "Will there be anything else, sir?"

Price waved the waiter away. The young reporter took a dollop of sour cream and placed it on the neatly split baked potato. Price helped himself to the asparagus, and then offered several spears to Miller, which he accepted. For several minutes, they focused on their meals. As the professor had promised, the food was exquisite. The reporter—more used to Chinese takeout or grabbing a sandwich at the deli—allowed himself to enjoy every bite. There was no telling when he might have a meal like this again.

Price sampled the swordfish, the rice, and the asparagus, but clearly was eager to continue his narrative. When Miller did not provide the opening to renew the conversation, he took it on his own. "I knew I would have to go back to meet her."

"Meet who?"

"Alison. Henry's daughter. If anyone might have a clue to his disappearance and his whereabouts—or whenabouts—it would be her. Before I continue, though, there were two details to take care of. First, I jumped to 2008 and read up on Obama. I realized trying to place long term bets in 1997 on some obscure Illinois state legislator was only going to call attention to myself, especially when they paid off. Instead, I started carefully placing my bets after his keynote speech at the 2004 Democratic National Convention, and made larger bets spread out over the next three years. By the time he got the nomination in 2008, the odds were so in his favor it was hardly worth it."

Miller cut off a piece of his potato and dipped it in the juices on his plate. "I hoped you thanked him for your good fortune."

"Oh, I did. I was the one who started the grass roots movement to get Sarah Palin on the Republican ticket."

The reporter looked at Price with his fork in midair. He shook his head. "You're pulling my leg." The professor maintained a straight face. "Okay, have it your way. What's the other thing you needed to take care of?"

Price smiled. "I was hoping you'd cut off a piece of your prime rib so I could have a small taste."

OFFICE ROMANCE

As I entered the building I automatically looked at the directory. It was 1977, and Alison Gondelman had been working on her father's papers for nearly a year while she was also teaching some introductory classes. She had gotten her Masters, but apparently her heart wasn't in research or otherwise succeeding on the tenure track, so she took the assignments more senior faculty had no interest in. Everyone understood that her most valuable contribution would be sorting through the papers and seeing if there was anything unpublished that should be brought to light. At the very least, organizing the documents for the university archivists would be a major accomplishment in and of itself. She had an important role to play, and she was playing it well. Of course, to go through her father's papers meant she required the obvious room assignment. Once again, I walked into my own office, and once again, someone was startled. To my annoyance, it was me. Again. It was getting to be a habit.

"It's about time you got here," she said. She had long dark hair that she pulled back and tied into a bun. She wore big, dark-framed glasses that were much bigger than they needed to be, but reflected the current style. I was instantly smitten. Her white lab coat was unbuttoned, and hung loosely over a tie-dyed T-shirt and blue jeans. The shirt was apparently from some concert she'd attended, although the name on it was meaningless to me. What I got, instead, was that she had been expecting my arrival, and was annoyed that I had arrived at that moment.

"You were expecting me?"

She sighed. "Yes, Willy, of course I was expecting you. My father told me all about you. I know you're from the future and that you helped him complete his work in temporal mechanics."

Well, it would be nice not to have put on an act for her, but what did she actually know about me? Gondelman's notes had mentioned nothing about telling his daughter anything. It was only when I did my research in 1997 that I discovered she had been officially named curator of her father's papers in 1976. I showed up in 1977, figuring it would take a year or so just to get a handle on her father's work and, perhaps, discover my role in it. Apparently, I was wrong.

I closed the door and walked into the office. It looked pretty much the same, except for some new shelving by the windows holding several open cartons. One was labeled "Personal," another "Administrative," and a third "Miscellany." The topmost shelf had three boxes, all marked "Temporal Mechanics." On the seat next to the desk was a fourth one marked the same. I moved it to the floor and sat down.

"Since I was expected, I might as well make myself at home," I looked at her and extended my hand. "Hello, I'm Wilford Price, a friend of your father's. Pleased to meet you."

She looked at me for a long moment, and then finally took my hand. Her face broke out into a smile. "I'm sorry, I guess that was rude of me. I'm Alison Gondelman. I'm very pleased to meet you." She took my hand and held it for a few beats longer than necessary. When she finally let go, she said, "What time did you come from?"

"1997. That's where this is *my* office and—"

"No, I meant what time of *day* did you come from? I've been here since early this morning, and I'm ready for lunch. Would you like to join me?"

If I was there strictly on business, I suppose I could have just jumped forward an hour or two, but I had skipped breakfast myself. "Delighted," I said. "Where did you have in mind?"

"It's a beautiful day. I thought we might go down to the river."

It turns out she was not suggesting I catch our lunch, not that I would eat anything that actually came out of the river the school sat beside. There's a local beer that carries the same name as the river, and students used to joke that it was so toxic they simply bottled the water untreated. Instead, we first walked over to the food court at the then-new student union nestled on the other side of the academic quad.

"It just opened last year," she said of the massive cube of glass, steel, and brick. "There was a big celebration. Quite a bit of fuss."

I knew it in my time as a twenty-year-old building where they had just torn out the entire student lounge in the atrium and redone it. We walked down to the basement level food court. I picked up a salad garnished with grilled chicken, she took a blueberry yogurt. I offered to pay, but she touched my arm as I reached for my wallet. "Don't be silly," she said. "Dad would insist."

"Actually, what your father offered me was some leftover cheese and crackers and a tumbler of scotch."

"No scotch, I'm afraid. You'll have to make do with that," she said, indicating a refrigerated case filled with sodas and juices.

I reached for a green bottle of Perrier. "Not much of a selection of water."

She gave me a funny look as she picked out a hot pink can of Tab. "Why would there be a selection of water? Don't you have indoor plumbing in your time?"

We suspended our conversation as the bored cashier rang us up. Then Alison led us over to the counter with the straws, napkins, and plastic utensils. "The past is a foreign country: they do things differently there," I quoted.

It took a moment. "*The Go-Between*," she said. "I loved that movie. Have you ever read the book?"

"I'm afraid not." In fact, I only knew the movie because I had taken a college film class to fulfill a distribution requirement, and the professor had had a lifelong crush on Julie Christie. Alison threw what we needed into the plastic bag containing our lunches, and took my arm.

"Let's head to the river. It's too noisy to talk here, and too nice a day to stay inside. Follow me, I know just the spot."

We emerged outside and walked past the older student dorms and the fraternity quad as we headed toward the river. It was mild and sunny out. I would often drive by this area on my way to the faculty parking lot, but I don't know if I had ever actually walked around there. She led the way to a bench shaded by a large elm tree. We could hear the water flowing by and, off in the distance, the traffic from the road on the other side of the river.

As she handed me my salad and fork, she said, "I love sitting here on a nice day and watching the river. It's so peaceful."

"Indeed, just like the stream of time." I was trying to be poetic. I was hoping I didn't sound like a lovesick freshman.

She carefully removed the cover of her blueberry yogurt, depositing it in the bag. Then she stirred up the fruit from the bottom, methodically mixing it all together. Finally satisfied that the fruit was evenly dispersed throughout, she stopped stirring and looked at me. "So, tell me Willy, what's the future like?"

"You mean do we have flying cars and jet packs?"

"No," she said. "I mean is it a better world? Have you eradicated disease? Eliminated hunger? Ended war? Wiped out racism?"

My fork was halfway between my salad and my mouth, and I froze midway. "That's quite a lot of things you expect us to solve in just twenty years."

"Is it?" She took a sip of her diet soda. "Suppose someone from the late 1940s showed up today. He'd be amazed that we conquered polio, ended segregation, and helped rebuild a Europe devastated by the war. Why shouldn't I have high expectations for the future?"

I let myself swallow before answering. "Well, that's not really fair."

"Why not?"

"Well, for one thing, you gave yourself an extra decade."

"You're good," she said, with a laugh. "Were you on the debating team?"

"No, but I can do the math in my head." I went on to tell her about the world of 1997. Some things were better and some things were worse. She gasped when I described the outbreak of AIDS, which might already be present in her world, only no one knew about it yet. Like her father, she was fascinated at the concept of personal computers, especially ones that could be easily moved from place to place.

"It sounds like it's much the same. There are changes in the details, but I'd probably fit in your world without missing a beat." She paused to put her empty soda can and yogurt cup in the bag. As she reached for my now-finished salad container, she said, "Do you think I might see it?"

I instinctively clutched my briefcase. Was this whole family obsessed with time travel? "I'm afraid I don't have a spare time machine to offer you. In fact, when I—or a future version of me—tried to give one to your father, it was a miserable failure."

"I know," she answered. "And don't worry, I'm not going to try to steal your device. I'm simply curious. Do you think it would be able to transport us both?"

Now that was an interesting question. So far as I knew, the device was a single passenger machine. The ones I knew of had been used only by me except, of course, for the one her father had built. I had some indication it was a somewhat more available bit of equipment at some unspecified time in the future, but that didn't answer the question. "I don't really know," I replied. "I haven't tried to conduct any experiments transporting anyone other than myself."

She stood up and walked over to a nearby trash barrel to deposit the remains of our lunch. Alison then looked back and made it clear she was expecting me to follow. "Well, what are you waiting for? Let's find out."

We headed back to my/her/Henry's office. It was mid-afternoon. The sounds and sights on the academic quad were the same as they'd be in my time, with allowances made for changes in hairstyle and fashion. I thought of mentioning that one of the biggest breakthroughs in my time was that we had rediscovered hairstyles that didn't make us look ridiculous, but I didn't want to be… what would the word be, "timist?" I thought the facial hair configurations back in the 1860s were pretty outrageous as well. I suspect it has a lot more to do with what you're used to seeing every day than anything else.

We stopped by the department office for Alison to check her mail. There was no e-mail yet, and departmental and university notices still cost the lives of several trees each day. Alison said hello to a colleague, and I was startled to realize it was a twenty-years-younger version of Dr. Surkis, then an associate professor who was well on her way to full tenure. I started to greet her, but caught myself. The me in this timeline was only seven years old. She wouldn't know me. She gave me a funny look as I tried to make myself inconspicuous. If this time travel device ever became widespread, there would have to be a lot of warnings about potential paradoxes in the user's manual.

When we got to her office and shut the door, we could finally speak freely. I told her I thought it was a bad idea to overload the time travel device for all the obvious reasons. "I'm still working out how it operates. Even with your father's insights, I don't know if I can create a large enough…," I stumbled for the word, "Zone? Aura? Whatever?—that will encompass us both. And obviously I can't let you take the machine on your own, even if Time permitted it. If something went wrong, you'd be stranded in the future and I'd be stuck here. That clearly isn't acceptable, and I doubt we'd be allowed to let it happen."

While I made my little speech on why she couldn't travel to the future, she was moving boxes and chairs around the office, creating an empty space in the middle of the room. "Willy, I'm not suggesting you try to give me the device, or that I try to take it. I'm not even suggesting I travel to your time… at least not yet. What I'm proposing is an experiment. We're scientists. We do experiments, remember?"

As I watched, she kicked a box toward the back of the office. "Okay, I'm listening. What are you proposing?"

She put on her lab coat. "This makes it more scientific," she said with a grin. I had to admit I was finding her smile infectious. Now understand, I fully respected and supported my female colleagues since I was coming from the more enlightened time of 1997. My department chair was a woman. Women were and are major contributions in the field. But this wasn't about "women" or even "women physicists." This was about one woman and my responding to her as one man. However I simply kept my thoughts to myself. I engaged in what people were starting to call "multitasking." One part of my brain focused on our professional and academic discourse, another part recognized the tie between us because of her father, and another part—the part I was holding sharply in check—was wondering if she would consider dating a man from another time. While I was processing all this, I realized she had been talking. Apparently I wasn't particularly good at this multitasking. I asked her to repeat herself.

"I'm suggesting we travel one day into the future together. That shouldn't overtax the device or disrupt the time stream."

"No, it shouldn't. But how do you propose we travel together? As far as I know, the device is personal to me."

She had me take it out and set it for twenty-four hours from now. "Now just hold on a moment." She then indicated I should step into the space she had created in the center of the office. I took a few steps forward. She did the same, put her arms around my neck, and stepped in so close that there was virtually no space between us. "Hit the 'go' button, or whatever it is."

I was so startled at her proximity—I could smell the floral scent in her hair—that I just did as she asked. There was a brief stutter, and then nothing. She stepped back. I looked at the clock. It was still five past two.

"Did it work?" she asked.

"I don't know." The office looked exactly the same, of course. It felt different, though, and it took me a moment to put my finger on it. It was quiet. I turned and opened the office door. The hallway was empty. "Where is everyone?"

Alison joined me at the door. "If it's Saturday, they're all home or in the library or the dorms, or wherever they go on a Saturday afternoon."

"How do we know it's Saturday afternoon?"

"One way to find out," she said, slipping out of the lab coat and then taking me by the arm. I grabbed my briefcase and slipped the device inside. We were soon outside the building, but the presence or absence of student foot traffic told me nothing. She took me past the library and toward one of the dorms.

As we crossed the road at the back of the library, I began to realize what her "proof" was. We heard the roar of the crowd before we saw it. As we got closer to the dorm, she pointed to our left. I may have had little contact with the school beyond my classes and departmental matters, but I knew what a college football game sounded like. Down below the hill where the dorm was, we could see that the stadium was half-filled—we weren't a big sports school—and our team and some other team were scrimmaging on the field. I couldn't be sure which was our team, although I assumed the blue and yellow uniforms were indicative of our school colors. It didn't matter. Games were played on Saturday afternoon, not Friday. We had gone a day into the future.

"We did it! We've travelled together." I was ecstatic. She smiled, but the smile quickly vanished from her face. Instead, she looked panic stricken. "What? What is it?"

"We have to get to my house, immediately."

"What's the matter? What's wrong?" I wondered what horrible outcome she had failed to anticipate.

"If this is really Saturday afternoon, then no one fed Spock this morning."

She was making no sense. "Spock? Who's Spock?"

"My cat. Hurry, let's go."

The modest but nicely appointed house was only ten minutes away from the university. Spock, a black and white tabby, had been left plenty of dry food and water, but was used to having a fresh can opened for him every morning. He greeted Alison with a loud, "Meow!" He gave me a look that indicated "I'll deal with you later," and trotted off ahead of her into what I presumed was the kitchen. As she opened the can whose label indicated it was filled with "mixed grill entrée," whatever that might be, Spock was doing figure eights around her ankles. Clearly she was going nowhere until he was fed. When she placed the bowl down, I could hear the purring across the room.

"Cats are creatures of habit," she explained, as we left the fur-covered vacuum cleaner to his own devices. As Alison washed up, I wasn't quite sure how to proceed, so I asked where the cat's name came from. She looked shocked. "Mr. Spock. From *Star Trek*. Surely you still have *Star Trek* in the future."

I didn't go in much for mass entertainment, but of course I had watched it from time to time. "Yes, but I can't keep track of all the different television series and movies. I think there are two or three different ones going on at the moment."

Her eyes went wide. "Really? You're getting *new* episodes?"

"Sometimes I get them mixed up with *Star Wars*..." I started to say, and she rolled her eyes. "I know there's more than one new television show, and I think the old actors have been making movies. You really can't escape it."

"Why didn't you tell me this earlier? So things really do get better in the future." I began to wonder if I should be worrying about her mental stability when she laughed. "Don't worry. I'm not a Trekkie. I have a life. It's just that all we have now are reruns from the 1960s. When do these new movies and TV shows start?"

"I'm sorry, I really don't know." I had seen a few of the movies when I was a kid, so I knew it had to be soon. "I don't think you'll have too much longer to wait."

"That's the third most exciting thing to happen to me this week," she said, as we stepped out of the kitchen and into the living room. When she didn't elaborate, I had to ask what the others were. "Why, meeting you and travelling through time. I'm still not sure which is number one, though." She gave me a grin that indicated she was just teasing. Apparently, I was someone worth teasing.

"I've probably taken up enough of your time for our initial meeting," I said. I reached into my briefcase for the time device, and noticed something odd. A red light that I hadn't previously noticed was furiously flashing to the right of the controls.

Alison noticed this too. "What does that mean?"

"Beats me. It hasn't done that before." I looked the device over, and found a little brass plate on the side with some writing on it. I removed my glasses and—squinting—could just make out the words which I read aloud, "Do not use when red light is flashing."

"You think we overtaxed it? Maybe it needs to cool off or recharge or something."

"Well, whatever it is, it looks like I'll have to stay in 1977 for a while. Maybe I should go back to campus…"

"Don't be silly," said Alison. "Do you have some appointment you have to make? Time travel should mean that you're always on time."

"I just don't want to impose…" I began.

"Relax, Willy. It's too early for dinner, but there's no reason we can't sit in the back yard and get to know each other a bit more. Since we're going to be working together, it seems like the right thing to do." Suddenly she started to laugh.

"What?"

Alison said, "I've just had a great idea for a book. We've travelled a whole day into the future. To us, it seems like we just finished lunch a little while ago, but in fact we haven't eaten since yesterday. We've missed Friday dinner, and breakfast and lunch today. And yet I don't feel the least bit hungry. I think *The Time Travel Diet Book* could be a big best seller."

"I don't think it works that way. It's not like you've fasted for twenty-four hours. You just skipped over those meals."

I got that look again. "Willy, I was joking," she smiled to take the sting out of her chiding. "We can have dinner in a few hours. Right now? Let me show you what a lazy Saturday afternoon is like in 1977. Why don't you get a couple of glasses out of the cabinet over there, and I'll open up a bottle of something. You do drink, don't you?"

"I have a preference for single malts," I volunteered.

"Sorry, I'm fresh out of ice cream. Will a German white wine do?"

I fetched the glasses while she pulled a bottle out of the fridge and smoothly uncorked it. We headed out to the back yard, which had two chaises already opened on a little cement patio that abutted a mini-garden. There was an elm tree which had begun to shift to autumnal colors, a bit of grass—one would hardly call it a "lawn"—and some bushes and flower beds. Alison filled the glasses halfway and took one, placing the bottle between us.

"So since you're from the future, I assume you know all about me," she said.

"Actually, I know even less about you than I do about *Star Trek*. You father mentioned that you were in college, and when I discovered his disappearance and returned to my own time, the news articles simply mentioned a daughter who would be going through his papers on behalf of the university. You probably know a lot more about me."

She took a sip of the white wine. "All I know is what my father told me. You're from the future. You have a time machine. And he enjoyed working with you because you were more into applied physics than theory, which was his field. Oh, and you would have his office someday."

Clearly, we had details to fill in. I told her about getting the time machine from my future self, and my adventures and misadventures testing it out. I told her about the strange circumstances of meeting with her father, and how shocked I was when he disappeared. When I came across a report that she started teaching in 1976 while going through her father's papers, I decided to travel to 1977 in order to give her some time to get a handle on the project. I had no idea how much she knew. It turned out to be quite a bit.

She refilled our glasses. "This is going to take a while," she said. "It's a complicated story."

"That's okay," I said, by way of encouragement. "Since I met my future self, complicated has become a way of life for me."

We understood each other. "Dad and I were close, but it required me to take him on his own terms. My mother died when I was very young, and he was not the most warm and cuddly person. Yet he accepted the responsibility of raising me, and gave me his support and his love. I always knew he would be there for me. So I was very surprised when he showed up in Ohio in the spring of my junior year of college to tell me he'd be leaving."

"That would be in the spring of 1972?"

"Yes, I later figured out it was between your first and second meetings. He had just sent his manuscript off to the publisher—the one with the chapter on temporal mechanics—and he told me he had to go away. I didn't understand, but he explained about you coming to see him and learning that time travel was real. He had devoted his whole life to the subject, and had to see for himself. He told me he loved me very much, that I would have a good life, and that we would see each other again. Then he said one of the reasons we would be apart for some time was because there were things I had to experience on my own without any warning or preparation."

"Really? Did he explain what he meant?"

"No, he said he couldn't. He said that I would meet a young man from the future—apparently that would be you—and that I was to trust you and let you have complete access to his work. And he said that while it would be a long time before we would be allowed to see each other again, he would be watching over me and making sure I wasn't left on my own."

"'Allowed?' That was the word he used?"

"Exactly. I didn't really understand it, but it's not like he gave me much time. After he told me what he had to say, he embraced me and said, 'Until we meet again.' And then he left. I haven't seen him since. Yet I know he's been watching over me."

"Wow. That's quite a story," I said. It was as bizarre as my journey, if not more so. "Have you heard from him since?"

"Yes and no. The following year, I graduated college, and it was a bittersweet day. I got my diploma, but I had no one there to witness it. When I got home, there were two things waiting for me. One was a letter from the university president pointing out that my father had been missing for over a year and was presumed dead. Under state law, we would have to wait three years to have him legally declared dead. In the meantime, the university offered me immediate acceptance into their graduate program —tuition-free—if, upon conference of the degree, I would take on the project of organizing Dad's papers."

"What was the other thing?"

"A letter from Dad urging me to accept the offer. He apologized for not being able to attend the graduation, but included a present. It was a silver bracelet that had belonged to my mother. He said she would have been proud of me and would want me to have it. Then he added that at some point in the project of sifting through his papers, I'd meet you."

Alison stopped, but I didn't know if that was the end of the story or the place where she didn't know how to continue telling it. "And what happened then?"

"I accepted the offer, and finished my Masters in 1976. Technically, I was then supposed to be pursuing my Ph.D., but at that point both the university and I knew I was really there to go through Dad's papers. So I focused on that, and taught the introductory courses that the senior faculty had lost interest in long ago."

The sun was heading toward the horizon. Alison refilled our glasses, emptying the bottle. "And waited for me?"

"Dad had told me you'd show up, but he hadn't said when. So for the last year, every knock at the door made me wonder if this was it."

I think I may have blushed. "I'm so sorry. If I had any idea, I would have come sooner. I wanted to give you time to get a handle on his papers."

"It's okay. I understand."

"It would have been just as easy for me to pop up a year ago…"

Alison raised her nearly empty glass. "It's okay, Willy. You did what you thought was right. In fact, I don't know that I disagree. Look, let me start dinner. Why don't you see how the device is doing?"

We headed back inside. Alison took the empty bottle and glasses, and I headed toward the time machine. The red light was stilling flashing. "Not leaving any time soon."

"Then please stay for dinner. I hope you like chicken and rice." She proceeded to toss together a simple Japanese dish involving chicken, rice, soy sauce, and scallions. "It's simple, but it has lots of protein. Not a bad thing after a day of time travel and emotional shocks."

We made small talk while she cut up the chicken and set the rice to cook. I don't recall what it was. It had been an amazing twenty-four hours or so. Longer, actually, if you counted the day we skipped. I think we both need to relax. When she served dinner, she asked if I would like chopsticks.

"Please," I replied. "It was a hard-won skill, and I've worked to maintain it."

"Great. I like a man who knows how to handle his tools."

Hello? What was that? Was she flirting with me? I gave her an uneasy grin. "You know, I could take that one of two ways."

"I'm sure. But I only meant it one way."

I'd never been very good at getting the signals young people sent each other to indicate romantic and/or sexual interest. I didn't understand it in

1965 visiting my father, and I understood it even less now in 1977. That probably explained why I was still single in 1997. "You make it worth handling," I said, having no idea if that was an appropriate response, but unable to think of anything else.

After dinner, I helped her clean up and checked the time device again. The red light was still flashing. We stood in the kitchen, and I wasn't sure what to do or say. "Looks like you're spending the night," she said.

I coughed. "I didn't bring my pajamas."

"That's so cute. I still have my dad's pajamas, but that might be a bit much…"

I made a face indicating that wearing Henry's pajamas while spending the night with his daughter was *not* my idea of a good time. "I don't think so."

"It's okay. The guest room is all made up, and I can lock my own door," she said with a sly smile. "And I make a great breakfast."

We headed upstairs. "I have no idea how long this will last."

"Don't worry about it. We'll deal with it the morning," she said, as she handed me a set of guest towels and an unused toothbrush. "When I arrived to work on my Masters, I had no idea where I would live. That's when I received an envelope with no return address that provided me with the deed to my father's house, dated a year before he disappeared. It was being held by a trust in my name. Haven't had much company since, but he did leave me prepared."

She showed me to the guest room. "I guess this is good night."

"It's been a very good night," Alison said as she kissed me on the cheek. "You might want to close your own door, unless you want Spock conducting his own investigation while you sleep."

I woke up, dressed, found the bathroom down the hall, and washed up as best I could. I came downstairs to the smells of breakfast, with Alison cooking up a storm.

"Good morning. I usually just have some cold cereal or an English muffin, so thanks for giving me an excuse to show off," she said by way of greeting. "Mr. Coffee has a fresh pot on the counter by the window."

I was wondering if she had invited another guest for breakfast, and then saw that "Mr. Coffee" was a home brewing system. I fixed myself a mugful and, after a sip, was ready to greet the new day… which had, in fact, occurred twenty years ago in my past. Alison was spooning batter onto a griddle contraption. "Is that Mr. Waffle?"

"Did you sleep well?"

"Well enough. What is all this? You didn't need to make a whole production for me."

Alison watched the indicator on the waffle iron to see when it was time to release its captives. "I used to do this for my Dad. It's been a long time. Let me enjoy myself. Have some fresh squeezed orange juice while you're at it. And if you want to be helpful, you can warm up the maple syrup. It's in the fridge." I opened the refrigerator and saw a bottle of syrup. It wasn't a brand name syrup with a hint of maple flavoring. It was a bottle of New York syrup graded Light Amber. "Nice. I love real maple syrup."

"We're in the northeast. Why should we accept anything less than the real thing?" she said, pouring the last of the batter onto the waffle iron surface. She closed it, and it made a satisfying hiss. "Fill the pourer on the counter, and stick it into the microwave for fifteen seconds. I just got it."

"The pourer?"

"The microwave, silly. The prices have really come down. In your time, you probably have one in every room of your house."

I set the timer for fifteen seconds and shut the door. "No, we find one in the kitchen and one in the bathroom usually suffices."

She gave me a funny look. "The bathroom...?"

"For warming up the toilet seat on cold winter mornings."

She laughed. "You have a terrible poker face."

"Your father had the same reaction," I said. The timer dinged, and I used an oven mitt on the counter to transfer the container to the table.

"Waffles are ready. Dig in," she said, bringing the platter to the table. We talked about this and that, me in the clothes I had first put on Friday morning, and she in pajama bottoms and another T-shirt from a concert featuring yet another band unknown to me. I don't recall much of what we talked about, until the conversation took a serious turn when I mentioned how my father had died before I had gotten to know him.

"If I ever become a father, I'm going to be very nervous. It's not like I've had someone to serve as a role model for me."

"And I'm the classic motherless daughter. Dad was a good father, but I ended up playing the substitute mommy. I did a lot of the household chores as I got older, and often had to remind him that he might want to shave before a big meeting with alumni who were major donors. There were times that I think I was the one raising him, rather than the other way around."

"Well, it can't be easy being a single parent," I said, mopping up the last of the syrup on my plate with the final bit of waffle. "Do you plan on having children?"

She stood up and started clearing the table. "Please, Willy, we just met."

I was chagrined. "I'm sorry. I didn't mean that we…"

"I'm joking," she said with just a touch of exasperation. "You're as bad as my father. No wonder the two of you want to travel in time. The modern age must constantly baffle you."

"I'm not *that* bad, am I?"

"Let me finish up in here. Go check the time device and see if I'm going to have to start figuring out what to make you for lunch."

A few minutes later, she met me in the living room with a large padded envelope. I was sitting on the couch, idly petting Spock. The cat purred and rubbed against me, accepting the attention as his due. "It's because of the pointed ears, isn't it?"

"What is?"

"You named the cat Spock because he has pointed ears."

"I can see why they awarded you a Ph.D. You actually figured that out in less time than it took my Dad. Do you know that for years he thought it was for Dr. Spock, the baby doctor?" She sat down beside me, and Spock jumped off, apparently deciding his attention was needed elsewhere. "Is the red light off?"

I pulled the device out of my briefcase. It was indeed off. "I guess that means I can go home." I didn't really want to leave, but I remembered a friend in college quoting an old show business axiom, "Always leave them wanting more." Meaning: don't overstay your welcome.

She must have read something on my face. Apparently I broadcast my feelings in the same way the proverbial space aliens were getting our *Star Trek* reruns. "It's okay," she said. "It's only *au revoir*, not *adieu*. Until we meet again. But before you go, there's something I'd like you to take with you." She handed me the package. "It's my father's notebooks related to his work with you. I think you should take some time to go through them before we continue working together."

"Thanks." I opened the envelope. There were two thick notebooks inside. I started to flip through them.

She put her hand on my arm. "You'll have plenty of time for that when you get home. Take them with you and take all the time you need. The first one is filled with his notes and calculations for the chapter in his book on temporal mechanics. It's the second one you'll want to examine closely. It's all the material he decided *not* to include in the book."

I had a sudden thought. "You know, the device makes time elastic for us. I can spend a day, a week, even a whole year going through the material, and then come back in time to five minutes from now."

"And not even give me time to shower?"

"Well, I didn't mean…"

She gave me the look that I was coming to understand meant, "It was a joke." Then she got serious. "I gave this some thought this morning, and I saw that that was possible. I also think it would be a mistake. I need time to process this, too. What's the hurry?"

"I guess I didn't think it through."

"This is new for both of us. Dad was the theorist, you're the applied science guy. I'm more interested in the philosophy of science. What does it mean? How will it impact our lives? It's the stuff you guys never really think about before unleashing your new discoveries and inventions on the world, leaving it to all the rest of us to muddle through as best we can after the fact."

I put the notebooks back into the envelope, and the envelope into the briefcase. "I don't know that that's fair."

"Really? When Edison invented the light bulb, did he think about how the electric light would impact astronomy? In many large cities now, you can barely make out the night sky. Did you know that when they did the first test of the atomic bomb, no less than Edward Teller speculated that it was possible that it might ignite the atmosphere? Scientists rush in where angels fear to tread."

I started to sit down. "Tell me more. This sounds like the start of a very stimulating conversation."

"Not today, Willy. Go read the notebooks. We can meet for lunch in our office next Friday."

"*Our* office?"

"We'll be spending a lot of time together there, and it *will* be your office eventually. So there's plenty of time for us to get stimulated in the future," she said with a smile. "Which reminds me: on your next visit, bring an overnight bag. You know, your shaving kit, change of clothes, whatever."

"Okay. Let me adjust the machine for both place and time, since I don't want to shock whoever lives here in twenty years, in case it isn't you." When I finished, I put out my hand. "It's been a real pleasure."

She ignored my hand. Instead, she stepped in close and gave me a kiss. "And, Willy, don't bother packing your pajamas."

Before I could react to that, she pressed the activation button on the device and quickly stepped back. The last thing I saw was the grin on her face.

NOTEBOOKS

Price let out a belch and put down the glass of seltzer. "Excuse me. I'll be fine. Sometimes I can get away with a bit of red meat. I think I made it through this one just under the wire." He called the waiter over to clear their dishes. "Coffee for me. Max?"

"The same."

"Would you like to look at the dessert menu?" the waiter inquired.

Price favored him with a smile. "It never hurts to look."

"Very good. I'll be back with your coffees in a minute."

When they were alone again, the reporter gave Price a "just between us guys" smile. "So, Gandalf's daughter was a real hottie, huh?"

"Gondelman," he corrected. "And she had a brilliant mind that came at problems from a very different angle. She was also, um, not unattractive."

"Willy, you sly dog, you."

Price looked for the waiter with the coffee. Clearly, there would need to be a bit of sobering up before heading back to campus. "So, other than your charming interest in my love life, do you have questions about anything else?" said the professor, trying to steer the conversation in the direction he wanted. "Say, about what was in those notebooks?"

Miller took a sip of water. "Okay, what was in those notebooks?"

"I'm glad you asked," replied Price. "The first notebook was precisely as she had described. It was filled with his notes and calculations that had led to the chapter I knew so well in his book. I quickly skimmed through it. I was touched where, in a few place, he noted my contribution."

"How did he do that?"

"He would write things like, 'Must thank Willy.' He really was very generous sharing credit, a trait that is not universal in my field."

The waiter arrived with the coffee service. He deftly poured the two cups from a small silver pot and then, just as quickly, headed off to his other tables. As the professor added his sugar and cream, Miller asked, "So other than a little egoboo, there wasn't much there?"

"Egoboo? Oh, I see what you mean. Yes, other than stroking my pride there wasn't anything there I didn't already know. I flipped through it in less than an hour. I would go back and study it later to see if I had missed anything, but I really hadn't."

Miller tried his coffee black, and then decided a drop of cream to cool it off would be okay. "All right," he continued, as he stirred, "so what was in the second notebook?"

"Ah, now that was really something." Price took a sip of coffee, as much for dramatic effect as anything else, and then set the cup down. "The second notebook was filled, as Alison had promised, with all the things he didn't feel comfortable putting in his book. Chief among the entries were a number of his ideas for improving the time travel device."

"Improve it? In what way?"

"A lot of it was technical and needn't concern us now. It was things like fine tuning the time and place controls, as well as getting advance readings as to whether a particular time was closed off to that traveler. Over the next few years, I began incorporating some of his ideas into the updated versions of the device. It's now at a point that the very existence of the device is a possibly unsolvable paradox."

"How so?"

"Allow me to recapitulate. My future self brought me a time machine in 1997 made with material and technology compatible with the era. I used it to go back to 1972, where Henry was able to figure out enough that—with the help of my cell phone—he was able to build a rudimentary device from the technology of *his* era. He left the notebook which allowed me to create improvements, which I've continued to do since then. The version I'm currently using is the fifth generation counting the 1997 version as time travel Device 1.0 and Henry's device as a prototype. Even though it came later in the process, it was first in the time line."

Miller was feeling dizzy, but at this point it was more from the explanation Price had just put forth than any lingering effects from the day's drinking. "I don't know if I quite follow all of that," he said. "But I see an obvious problem here."

"Yes," Price smiled, "What is it?"

"Where did the time machine originate? Who made the first one that set this whole process in motion?"

"Welcome back, Max," beamed Price. "Yes, that's precisely the question to ask, and I don't know that I have an answer to it. Henry had said we stood on each other's shoulders, and I don't know that he's wrong. At this point, the history of the Device is so knotted up that we might never be able to unravel it fully. However, figuring that out would soon prove to be the least of my concerns. I discovered I had a far higher priority."

"Getting back with Alison?"

Price rolled his eyes. "Yes, my boy, returning to see Alison was high on my agenda, but there was something else that would prove to be of slightly greater importance."

Miller couldn't quite hide his smirk. "And what would that be?"

Price replied with his own smirk as he finally played the ace that had been hidden up his sleeve for some time. "To find out what was in the third notebook."

It took a moment for the young reporter to process what he was hearing. "What third notebook? You said Alison only gave you two notebooks."

"That's right."

"So where did this third notebook come from?"

Price emptied half his coffee cup. "There might be hope for you yet, Max. Once again, you have zeroed in on precisely the right question."

SEX AND THE SINGLE
TIME TRAVELER

I had returned to my office in 1997. I suppose I could have set the coordinates to go straight home, but my car was in the faculty lot, so I thought I might as well return to campus. I took the envelope with Henry's notebooks and put it in the bottom drawer of my desk along with my scotch. Somehow, I think he would have approved.

Curious as I was to learn what was in the two books, I decided that Alison was right. We needed time to digest all that had happened and all we had learned since she and I had first met on Friday. We might be twenty years apart, but it was now Sunday afternoon for both of us, and there was a lot to consider. For one thing, Henry's papers were not completely available to scholars in 1997. There were a set of restrictions placed on a portion of them by the university for reasons I didn't quite understand, and for which little by way of explanation was forthcoming. Indeed, they would not be available to scholars at all for years to come. Instead of continuing to wonder what was there, I would now have complete and unfettered access to all of his papers.

Another thing that had happened was, quite obviously, meeting Alison herself. Almost from the moment I had first laid eyes on her, I found myself attracted to her and, as had become so obvious that even I couldn't miss it, she had become interested in me. Where was this going? Where *could* it go? She and I were young and healthy and in our twenties, but that was only if we ignored the fact that in her timeline, the non-traveling version of me had just started second grade. Could we ignore it? Would we be *allowed* to ignore it? I had no idea and, no doubt, neither did she. It's why she had wisely suggested that we both take some time to think about it.

However, right at that moment didn't seem quite the time for me to be thinking deep thoughts. It was too early for bed—it was barely lunchtime —but I could go home and take the day off. It had been my experience that the toughest problems became easier after I ignored them for a while and left them to my subconscious to handle. I'd come in Monday morning, bright and early, and tackle the notebooks and start considering where to proceed from here.

By lunchtime Monday, I had been through the first notebook, and seen enough of the second to know that I'd be spending a lot of time going over Henry's calculations and ideas. He raised some things that suggested to me ways that the time travel device might be improved, and still other things that were so out there that I couldn't quite grasp what he was getting at on a first read.

I replaced the two notebooks in their envelope, and secured it in my bottom desk drawer. When I left the office, I double checked to make sure the door was locked. I wasn't aware of anyone breaking into faculty offices, but one couldn't be too safe. It was the sort of material that mustn't be allowed to fall in the wrong hands.

I headed over to the student union. The atrium was a mess: the twenty-year-old furniture and fixtures of Alison's time was being carted out, and the area was being prepared for remodeling. I took the staircase downstairs and was startled for a moment. I rarely had reason to be in the student union, and for a moment was disoriented. Whoever had had the food service concession in 1977 had long since been replaced, and the entire area was different. After I got my bearings, I grabbed a turkey rollup and a bottled water (from a selection of half a dozen different choices) and thought about going down to the river. On second thought, no. It would only remind me that the Alison I knew was twenty years in the past. Who knew where the middle-aged Alison was today? That was a line of thought I chose not to pursue.

I stopped by the department office to pick up my mail. I smiled at Dr. Surkis, who was coming out of a meeting with the dean of the college. How democratic of him to come to her, rather than making her cross the quad over to him. She acknowledged my presence with a nod, and returned to her conversation. I slipped away and headed back down the hall to my office, which was still locked.

It took a few moments to carefully unpack my sandwich so that I could use the plastic wrap as a makeshift placemat on my desk. I opened my bottled water and placed it within reach. Now I could begin the process of puzzling out Gondelman's musings. I reached into my desk drawer and pulled out the envelope. When I opened it, I nearly lost all thoughts of lunch. Where I had left two notebooks not forty minutes ago, there were now three. I looked around the office to see if somehow there was someone else there, but I was completely alone.

Pushing aside my rollup, I took the three notebooks out. The first one was Henry's notes for the book. The second one was the one with the calculations that I had intended to study this afternoon. So what was this third one? Where had it come from? Well, there was only way to find out. I opened it and began reading.

Dear Willy (it read),

I'm glad you have finally starting going through my papers with Alison. I miss her more than I can say. Someday I'll get to see you both, but that will have to be sometime in the future. Right now, the best way for me to communicate with you is through this notebook. I slipped into your office while you were picking up your lunch, and dropped it off. Unfortunately, this is a one-way proposition. I won't see anything you jot in the notebook, but I will be able to send you the occasional message in the future (well, your future) when Time permits.

There's much I can't tell you. However I'm starting to see why I can't tell you. Some of it should be obvious. For example, when your future self tried to give me the time travel device, it was clearly disruptive of the time stream. I needed to understand it on my own, and I could only do that by building my own device and figuring out the principles under which it operated. When you gave me my book, seeing that it was a finished project gave me new knowledge—that I would complete it and it would be published—but I was not allowed to merely copy the material I had not yet worked out on my own.

The other thing I learned is, perhaps, less obvious. When I...

At this point, there was a blank space on the rest of the page. I could see the indentation where someone had attempted writing, as if he had been using a pen that had suddenly run out of ink. I tried to make out what was written there, but it was to no avail. I turned the page.

Apparently I'm not allowed to share that (it continued). *It's truly amazing how Time prevents things that are not meant to be.*

Okay. Let me see if I can convey this. You've got a lot of hard work ahead of you, and some tough times ahead. It will all work out. Have faith. We'll all meet again someday.

In the meantime, I'll be helping when and where I can.

Affectionately,

Henry

P.S. Let's keep this between ourselves. Please don't tell Alison I've been in touch with you.

"My father wrote to you?"

It was Friday afternoon in 1977, a week after I first met Alison. It was raining, so rather than head to the river, we were sitting side by side on the orange snaking couches in the atrium of the student union.

"And he told me not tell you."

She gave me a long, hard look. "And so you chose to betray his trust?"

I gave her an equally long and hard look. "I chose not to lie to someone that I've come to care about."

She looked back and finally said, "That is the sexiest thing that anyone has ever said to me." She leaned over and kissed me. And I kissed her back.

After a few moments, we separated and looked around. I was anonymous in 1977, but she was a member of the Physics faculty. Fortunately, none of her students seemed to be around.

"Alison, we can discuss our feelings later. My concern is your father. I only met him twice. You know the man. Is he stable? He tells me to have faith and we'll all be together some day. That sounds more like a sermon than a message from a man of science."

She took my hand. "I know my father. I trust him. But now I see I can trust you, too. I've also had a busy week."

It was obvious to me she had something to say. I put my other hand on hers, clasping them between mine. "Tell me."

"I also heard from my father."

"Did you see him?"

"No, but a few days ago, I discovered a notebook that hadn't been there before, just as you did. It contained a message from my father. He said he was watching over me, that he would make sure that I would not have to worry about money, and that even though there would be some bumps in the road ahead, it would all work out. Just as he did with you, he told me to have faith and that he would see me again someday."

There was a silence between us, and then we disengaged our hands. "What do you think it means?"

"I have no idea. I think all we can do is continue our work of sifting through his papers. You can hold on to the second notebook, or we can make a photocopy of it—if Time allows—as it sounds like that's what you need to examine in detail."

We got up, and disposed of our half-eaten lunches in a nearby receptacle. Walking through the tunnels back to the physics building, I knew that spending the afternoon in her/my/our office going through Henry's papers was the last thing I wanted to do. When we got there and closed the door, I took her in my arms and, for once, took the initiative. To my great relief, it was welcomed. When we came up for air, I looked at her and said, "Can we take some of these boxes to your house?"

She smiled. "There's no need to. There are boxes of his at home that we'll need to go through as well."

"No time like the present." In very short order, we were on our way.

We spent the afternoon going through several boxes of his papers. Gondelman was a pack rat. He had saved everything. A memo from 1965 about the use of the department mimeograph machine? He still had it. Student research papers from 1970? A whole stack of them. We went through every document and tried to determine its historic value. Most of the interoffice memos and student papers we trashed, but an exam from 1968 that got an A and a notation "You'll go far" we kept, just in case it turned out that she did go far. The letter informing Henry that he had been awarded tenure was kept, but the one telling him his parking space was being reassigned was not. Clearly, this was going to be an extremely long process.

Besides his academic files, there were also the truly personal papers. His own diaries from his student days. Letters between Henry and Alison's mother. Photo albums going back to his childhood. There was no question that these should be preserved. The question was whether they should be given to the university archives.

"I'll have to think about this. Dad didn't leave any instructions as to whether the school papers were to be all inclusive."

Remembering that not all his papers were available to me in my own time, I said, "You can restrict access to them. Not everything has to be made available to the public."

"How do you mean?"

"Well, Mark Twain dictated several volumes of autobiographical material with the proviso that they not be made public until a century after his death. For the most part, the material has remained under lock and key. It's not expected to see the light of day until 2010."

"Interesting. Let's see if Dad weighs in with an opinion before we're done."

She dropped a stack of papers in the box we were sifting through. "I think that's enough for today. Let's take the trash out and start thinking about dinner."

Taking out the trash took several trips, and soon filled the several pails in Alison's driveway. "I hope you'll be staying through Sunday night," she said. "It's not going to be easy to get these out to the street."

We headed back to the house, hot, tired, and sweaty. "I think I need a shower before I can even consider thinking about dinner tonight or taking the trash out on Sunday."

"Go ahead," she said. "Meanwhile, I'll figure out what we're going to do about dinner."

I headed upstairs and stripped. I had brought enough changes of clothes for the weekend, so I wasn't worried about running out of things to wear. Besides, I remembered helping my mother with the laundry when I was a kid. If it turned out that I had miscalculated, I wouldn't have to go down to the river and beat my shirt with a stick against a rock. I knew that I was more than able of handling the current era's laundry technology. I grabbed my travel kit and headed toward the bathroom. Alison had already left a set of towels on my bed, and I took that along as well. I left the kit and most of the towels on the counter by the sink, taking the wash cloth, soap, and shampoo with me into the shower. A few moments later, I was basking under a steady stream of hot water. I don't know what people did in the days before indoor plumbing, but that wasn't my concern. The day's grime and perspiration were washed away, along with my concerns about Henry's bizarre message from the future. Alison and I had agreed that honesty was the best policy, and that we would have no secrets. I was so relaxed under the spray of hot water that I didn't even notice when she slipped into the shower with me.

"Hi, sailor. New in town?" she said as slid behind me.

I turned around. "I suppose this would be a bad time for me to mention that I'm saving myself for marriage."

Her look of surprise lasted only a couple of seconds. "I don't think so," she said, as her hand slipped down below.

Two hours later, we were lying on the bed in the guest room, very much in need of another shower. "I'm guessing you won't be cooking tonight," I said, holding her close.

"I think that's a safe bet," she said, snuggling into my embrace.

Our hands idly explored each other's bodies, but at this point it was less something sexual than simply a sign of affection. I was even more exhausted then before, but in a good way. Running my hands along her curves was a way of reminding me that this was real. As for her touches, pleasant as they were, I doubted they were going to lead to a third engagement without a long respite. Having expressed ourselves sexually, this mutual touching simply said, "I'm enjoying being with you."

"You think your father expected this to happen?" I asked.

Alison moved back a bit. "Fascinating though it might be to speculate about that, I think I'd just as soon not be thinking about my father at the moment."

"Sorry," I said, realizing my gaffe.

She moved back in for a long, slow kiss. "I'm not."

I think we may have dozed for a bit. When I looked at the bedside clock, it was nearly 8 o'clock. I gently nudged Alison. "I think the time has come to decide if we're heading out or ordering in."

She smiled without opening her eyes. "What do you like on your pizza?"

"Not very much, I'm afraid. Is that going to be a problem? Are we going to break up over the fact that I don't like pepperoni?"

"You don't get out of it that easily," she said. "Can you handle mushrooms?"

"Mushrooms I can do."

"Hand me the phone."

I turned to the bedside table and grabbed the phone, which I put on my chest. She picked up the receiver and dialed the number from memory. "Hi, it's Alison Gondelman. I'd like to order a mushroom pizza.... Yes, that's the right address… Forty-five minutes? That's fine." She hung up the phone, which I returned to the nightstand. "Now, what can we do to occupy ourselves for forty-five minutes?" she asked.

"I just might have an idea."

It was actually closer to an hour later that we were downstairs with the pizza and a bottle of a chilled German wine. "I have a recipe I want to try out tomorrow night," she said. "Do you cook?"

"I'm afraid not. But I'm very good at cleaning up. It won't all be on you."

Alison laughed. "Willy, you need to relax. Enjoy yourself. I'm not constantly testing you."

I put down my glass. "I know, but I'm nervous. Except for that one time, I have no memory of my father and mother together. I have no model for this. You make me so happy that I don't want to do or say anything to mess it up."

Alison put down her half-eaten slice. "Willy, I get it. You're doing fine."

"Do you think your father anticipated this? Maybe he told us not to tell each other about hearing from him, knowing we would do it anyway and it would bring us closer together."

"And maybe he sent Cupid from the far future to shoot his magic arrows at us," she said. "I don't think trying to guess his motivation is going to get us very far. All I know right now are two things. First, it's going to take us months and months to sort through his papers to see what's there."

"Really? We seemed to make a big dent in them today."

Alison nearly choked on her pizza slice. "Dent? We've barely just begun. Why do you think I parked the car in the driveway? You know what the garage is filled with?"

"More boxes?"

"Not only more boxes. It's the overflow when he couldn't fit any more in the attic or the basement. We've only begun to explore the world of Henry Gondelman."

I laughed. Sure, it would be a lot of work. It would also mean a lot more time with Alison. "So, what's the other thing you know?"

"I can't imagine going on without you."

I think my heart skipped a beat. "I feel the same way," I said.

She picked up her wine glass and took a sip. She sighed, then looked at me. "Can we possibly have a future together? Do you have someone back in 1997?"

I met her sigh for sigh, and saw that made her nervous. "No, there's no one else," I hastily added. "As to whether we can have a future together, I have no idea. You and I are nearly the same age, but in 1977 the 'real' me is only a child. Can I be in love with someone who is, literally, old enough to be my mother?"

Alison looked at me. "Are you in love with me?"

I took a deep breath. "Yes, Alison, I am. I've never met anyone like you, and I haven't stopped thinking about you since we first met. And I don't know what to do about it or how we're going to make it work."

"Yet you came back."

"Yes, I came back. If I can't imagine how it works, I also can't imagine walking away from you."

She got up and started clearing the dishes. "Oh, no, you don't get away that easy," I said, taking her by the wrist. I kissed her. "And I meant what I said about cleaning up. It's not all on you."

"Okay," she said, "Since I didn't make dinner, we can both clean up tonight."

We stayed up late into the evening, but I don't recall that there was much more by way of serious conversation.

This was our schedule for months to come. I'd meet her on campus on Friday, and we'd spend some time going through his father's boxes that were stored in the office. Then we'd have the weekend at the house, going through the even larger collection of boxes that were there. Of course it wasn't all work, and neither of us was in any hurry to complete the project. In that sense, Henry's disorganization—or his peculiar sense of organization—was to our advantage, as it considerably slowed us down. He had not ordered the boxes by the nature of the material stored therein. Instead, it was strictly by when the box got filled up and put away. I suspect he knew he wouldn't be the one going through them, because it would have been difficult if not impossible to retrieve anything filed this way.

The box labeled "October 1969," for example, included copies of his syllabus for "Introduction to Physics," a 16mm film called "Our Friend, the Atom," flyers for something called "The Vietnam War Moratorium," which was apparently a protest *against* the war, and an invitation to the department Halloween party. Alison, who had been a freshman in college at the time, vividly remembered the protests of the era.

"Dad and I rarely discussed politics. I didn't even know that he took a position on the war."

"I learned a little bit about it in school. It was still too recent for the teachers, and we didn't spend much time on it."

Alison shook her head. "Amazing. So many lives lost in a war to contain communism, and a few years later, Nixon would go to China."

"I wonder what they would have made of the fact that the Soviet Union fell."

She looked at me in disbelief. "What did you say?"

"The Soviet Union collapsed of its own dead weight in 1991. The Berlin Wall came down. Germany was reunited. Vietnam's still communist, of course, as is China, Laos, Cuba, and North Korea, but that's about it. There was an academic who wrote about 'the end of history' about ten years ago, arguing that with the end of the Cold War, our global struggles were coming to an end."

Alison was astonished. "I have *got* to see the future."

We hadn't repeated our experiment from our first meeting. We decided the first priority was getting through the papers and then seeing if there was anything there that might help me boost the power of the device so that transporting two people didn't exhaust it. Moving the two of us a day into the future had caused it to shut down for hours. I had no idea what trying to travel together twenty years ahead would do to it.

When we weren't working, we were playing. I managed to bring back a portable VCR, and Alison and I were working our way through the *Star Trek* television episodes and movies. She quickly figured out that the even-numbered films were the good ones. The night I brought the first season of *Star Trek: The Next Generation*, she was torn between watching all of them non-stop, and ripping off my clothes and jumping me right in the middle of the living room. In the end, we managed to accommodate both of her desires.

By May, we had finished the boxes in the office and in the garage. We had had no more secret messages from Henry, and proceeded at our own pace. We were still deeply in love, which is why I was surprised when we had our first fight. It turned out to be a classic misunderstanding, even though the circumstances were such that they likely had never occurred before now. Alison and I were tracking each other twenty years apart. I'd spend weekends and holidays with her in 1977 and then 1978, while spending the work week back home in 1997 and 1998. This allowed each of us to get our mundane work done—preparing lecture notes and exams, grading papers—in the same time scheme. It seemed a natural way to do things, rather than my looking forward to summer while she was going through one of the worst winters she'd ever experienced.

Then in late April, I had a breakthrough with Henry's second notebook, and saw a solution to a problem that he had recognized and defined. The GPS could direct you to a specific location, but it didn't provide all the details of that location. I realized how lucky I'd been. Suppose I went to some place in the past or future, and the spot that was empty in my time now contained a filing cabinet or a boulder? What if I was going to a high rise, and the building had been torn down all together? Would my atoms appear within the object so that I'd be instantly killed? If I went to a tenth story office of a building no longer there (or not yet built), would I appear in mid-air and plummet to my death? The fix was a bit complicated, involving the projection of sonar into the time period ahead of the traveler, so that adjustments could be made for solid objects or the lack thereof. Of course, having the idea and making it work were two different things. The theorists always had the easy end of it.

I awoke on the Friday at the end of the week that I had started working on the problem, and as much as I missed Alison, I realized there was no reason I couldn't have my cake and eat it, too. I could go back to the Friday she was expecting to see me at any time. Instead, I worked through the weekend, and then right through the next weekend as well. Once I knew what I was doing, it turned out to be a relatively straightforward adaptation of the device, leading to what I came to think of as Device 2.0. (I had been using Device 1.1, with the original safely stored away.) After running a few tests on it, I was satisfied that the improvements worked. It was clear sailing now. With my grades in for the semester, I was now mostly on my own time until the fall semester. Since I no longer needed the income from teaching summer courses, I left them to my colleagues to squabble over.

It was Monday, May 18, in 1998, and I had missed two weekends with Alison. The dates didn't align exactly, and there were weekends when I was in one month in my time and the last month or next month in hers, but it worked out. And it would work out now. She was expecting me on Friday, May 5, 1978. Not a problem. I packed my bag, set the device for the time and place, and walked into what we now felt was our shared campus office. I was right on time, and she had no reason to suspect that for me it had been more than two weeks since I had last seen her. There was no reason to bring it up, really. What difference could it make?

The weekend went as planned. We worked, we cooked, we made love, we watched *Star Trek: The Next Generation* (I think we were up to the fifth season by now). It was as wonderful as ever. Late Sunday evening I said goodbye, as usual, only instead of setting the device to take me back to 1998, I simply skipped ahead a few days, to May 12, ready to pick up the next missing weekend where I had left off. It was win-win… until I walked through the door.

Alison was at her desk finishing up something, and smiled as usual. Then a strange look passed over her face, and she stood up. Instead of the usual welcoming hug, she looked at what I was wearing and said, "You've just jumped here from last Sunday, haven't you?" It hadn't occurred to me to go home and change my clothes. Who remembers what someone wore a few days ago? I don't. I barely remember what *I* wore a few days ago.

I tried to laugh it off. "Yeah, so I did. Couldn't wait to see you again."

"And you knew you were going to do that?"

I started to look sheepish. I didn't see what the big deal was. I was keeping to our schedule of seeing her each weekend. I said as much. "What's the problem?"

"Well, for one thing, you were pretending something that wasn't true. How is that different from lying to me?"

I was all set to get defensive and tell her she was being overly sensitive, but I caught myself. I sat down in my usual chair and dropped my bag on the floor. "I guess I didn't think it through. It didn't seem like an issue to me as long as I kept to your schedule. I got caught up in working on the device, and a couple of weeks slipped by, and I wanted to make them up."

"You could have told me."

"How? The device doesn't work on phone calls. And if I came back and told you in person, I wouldn't want to leave. I can see now how it seems like deception and, believe me Alison, hurting you was the last thing on my mind. In the future—and in the past, I guess—I'll let you know when my timing is out of sync with yours. Is that okay?"

She still wasn't smiling. "Willy, I appreciate that your intentions were good and you want to do the right thing. I'm not angry with you."

I smiled. "Well, that's a relief."

Her expression didn't change. "No, I'm angry with all of science."

Uh oh. "On behalf of the entire field—except for the chemistry department—can I just apologize for whatever we did and move on?"

She finally smiled, but it wasn't a happy one. "Of course you can. Just tell me what you did wrong."

This was getting worse. I suspected that no matter what I said, it wouldn't get at whatever was bothering her, and I would just be digging the hole deeper. "I surrender. Tell me what science did wrong by my wanting to make up my lost time with you."

"Ah, that's it," she said with satisfaction. "Now we can get at it. Remember how I told you I was much more interested in the philosophy of science than in the actual research? What it all means and how it affects our lives?"

"Yes, we started that conversation months ago and never followed up on it."

"Well, that was before you introduced me to Captain Picard. I had no idea bald men could be so sexy." She was smiling for real now. I started thinking that I was off the hook for any real or imagined wrongs but, no, there was still going to be a price to pay. The price turned into one of the strangest conversations I had yet had on time travel, and that was saying a lot.

"So how does my jumping over a week to get to the next weekend with you challenge science to its roots?"

She sat back in the chair, and it gave a little squeak. "I want you to imagine us in bed together."

"Are you sure you want to have this conversation here at the office?"

"Pay attention," she snapped. "This is about philosophy, not your animal urges."

I put on a wounded expression. "I thought you liked my animal urges. At least, that's what you said last weekend."

"Willy, I'm serious, and I'm asking you to take this seriously as well. It could have as big an impact on your work as my father's notebooks."

That got my attention. I thought this was all about beating me up a little more about my deception.

"Okay, professor, I'm all ears."

"All right. We've just made love and it was wonderful."

I smiled but said nothing.

She continued, "Now you get up and go to the bathroom to wash up. At least that's what you say. Instead, you use the device to travel back to your time. You take a shower and go to sleep. When you wake up several hours later you use the device to come back to my bathroom two minutes after you left it. To my surprise, when you return to bed, you're raring to go."

"I'm liking the sound of this, but I have an uneasy feeling that I'm not supposed to."

"That's right. You're not. A half hour later you're back in the bathroom, return to your time for two weeks, and then come back two minutes after you left. You're refreshed, and I'm turning into a rag doll. What's wrong with this picture?"

She stopped, clearly expecting me to reason out what the problem was. "Since we're being honest, let me start by saying that to the fifteen-year-old boy inside of me, there's absolutely nothing wrong with this picture. It's a fantasy come to life," I answered. Her reaction was not one of disapproval, but of waiting to hear what I was going to say next. I put up my hand so I could collect my thoughts. This was very important to her, and I was not going to get out of it with a glib answer. "Okay, to the adult academic who is so in love with you that it hurts, it is disrespectful. It's focusing entirely on my own needs, and treating you as an object without any feelings at all."

I thought that was the right answer, but until she graded it, I wouldn't know for sure. She got out of her chair and bent over me, giving me a big kiss. "A plus, Willy. That's it. What you did didn't rise to that level, but it was focusing on you without giving a thought to me. I know you meant well, and I'm not saying what you did was as bad as the hypothetical. In fact, I could have turned the hypothetical around and had me jumping through time to whenever you might be ready to perform. It's what Buber calls an 'I-It' relationship."

"Who?"

"Martin Buber. He was a philosopher. He said we relate to people in one of two ways: I-It and I-Thou. In the first mode, you treat the other person as an object, strictly in terms of how he or she serves your needs.

You stop someone on the street to ask for directions, you're not really interested in how he's feeling or what his life is like. You just want the directions. And an I-Thou relationship is what we have: the two people relate to each other as human beings. I care about you as a person, not simply as someone who can take out the trash or carry boxes upstairs…" and here she let me know all really was forgiven "…or satisfy me in bed, but as someone with hopes and dreams and a life that I want to share."

"And I feel the same way about you, Alison, except maybe that part about carrying boxes. I'm hoping that's eventually going to come to an end."

"I want to work out the ethics of time travel. Not simply what can or cannot be changed, or even what should or shouldn't be changed— although that will be part of it—but how we relate to each other when we're from different times. If you know I'm going to die next year, should you tell me? Should we be trying to set up rescue operations in the years before we know genocide will occur? And if we don't, are we moral failures?"

Now I was getting scared. "You got all that from me showing up in the same clothes?"

She laughed, and I knew the storm was over. "No, sweet Willy, I've been thinking about this since you first arrived. I think this may be where I can make my contribution to the study of temporal mechanics. Dad is the theorist. You focus on applied science. Eventually, there's going to be more than three of us who know about it, as you seem to have found out in the far future. Someone ought to be thinking about what it all means before it's too late."

"Whew. Okay, I don't have the answers to your questions, but I understand why not being up front with you was wrong, and I'm glad that we have such a strong relationship that we can be honest with each other without it getting ugly." I stood up and held her closely. "In fact, I love you more than ever."

Clearly, after this deep-dish discussion, we weren't going to accomplish much more at the office. I grabbed my bag and headed to the door. "Willy, where are you going? I don't want you to leave."

I spun around. "Oh, so now it's all about what *you* want. What about what *I* want?

She gave me a sly look. "Fair enough. What *do* you want?"

"I want to head over to your house and take a shower. I've been wearing these clothes all week."

THE NIGHT OWL

They had decided to skip dessert, and after Price settled the bill, the professor and the reporter found themselves out on the street. It was a pleasant evening, but the city had almost no nightlife to speak of, and the restaurant was far from the hotels and few clubs where there might have been some activity. That not only meant there was no one on the street, it meant there were no taxis anywhere in sight awaiting their business.

"I should have anticipated this," said Price, fumbling for his cell phone. "Let me call for a cab."

"Put your phone away, Willy," said Miller. "There's a cab stand a few blocks from here, near my newspaper's office. It'll give me a chance to stop by and check for messages. I can also leave a note for my editor not to expect me before noon tomorrow."

"All right," replied Price. "A little fresh air might do us some good."

They began walking through the darkened city streets. The street lamps provided illumination, but except for the occasional neon sign in a storefront window, it was like a ghost town. A municipal bus roared by, heading somewhere that didn't help them, but otherwise there was little in the way of traffic. The relative solitude allowed them to continue their conversation as if they were in private.

"You know," said Miller, "you make time travel seem a lot more complicated than in any of the books or movies I've encountered that use the concept. Usually, the character just presses the button and magically appears sometime in the past or the future, ready for adventure."

Price chuckled. "Real life is more complicated."

Miller tried not to roll his eyes, and nearly succeeded. "That assumes this cock and bull story you've been telling me all day is real."

"Just keep suspending your disbelief, Max. It will be worth your while in the end, I promise."

Miller sighed. "Okay. So let me ask you about Alison's philosophizing. Wasn't it a bit much? Weren't you just indulging your girlfriend because you had a good thing going?"

The professor shook his head. "Not at all. She was right. She was raising one of the least discussed but most immutable laws of science."

They reached a corner, where they were met with a harsh red "Don't Walk" signal. There were no cars approaching from any direction, and after just a moment's hesitation, they crossed against the light. "Okay, I'll bite," said Miller. "What law of science?"

Price smiled. "Why, the law of unintended consequences."

Price was about to explain when they stopped in front of the only office building that was showing any sign of life at this hour. "Here we are," said Miller. "Welcome to my world."

They slipped into the lobby. The only sound was the whir of a waxing machine one of the cleaning crew was using to polish the marbled floor. They walked carefully to the desk, where a bored guard accepted Miller's flash of an ID card and an indication that Price was with him. They both signed the night registry, and then Miller led them to the elevators.

Up on the fourth floor, the newsroom was hardly a hive of activity, but there were several reporters and editors working on the next morning's paper. There were stories to be written and copy to be edited and wire service reports to be gone through. Fortunately, none of that was Miller's concern.

"Hey Joe," he waved to the night editor, who waved back, and then returned to his task of cutting a report on a city council meeting in half. The reporter who had spent several hours of his life at the meeting and then writing it up would be howling in the morning when he saw his story in print, but by then, Joe would be home in bed and fast asleep. Miller led Price to his desk in the back. There were a few messages waiting for him, but nothing that required immediate attention, especially at this hour.

"Have a seat. There's a cab stand up the street when we're ready to head back to campus, but I suspect that you're ready to deliver another lecture, so I might as well be comfortable."

Price smiled as he sat down. "No lecture, Max, it's a simple fact. Actions in other times are no different from actions in our own time: they have consequences. And we can't always guess what those consequences will be. That's what Alison was telling me. Quite beyond the importance of not focusing selfishly on ourselves, there is also the need for us to recognize that what we do has an impact far beyond ourselves, and in ways we might not even be able to foresee. In fact, after my conversation with Alison, I had some of my grad students run a computer simulation to prove it."

Miller spun around in his chair to face to the professor. "You told them to model a time travel scenario?"

"No, of course not. I said I was exploring the ripple effects of changes in time, and wanted to see how much a single change would alter the course of history. To avoid tainting the research, I told them I would leave it up to them to pick some item of interest in history and to see how many things it would affect along the timeline if it were to be changed. My mistake turned out to be that I trusted this assignment to a bunch of nerds."

Once again, Price had hooked Miller, and Miller knew it. "Okay, you're a hell of a storyteller. Tell me what happened next."

"Three physics grad students tried to figure out what historic turning point they could study to see if things had turned out differently if they changed it. They decided to focus on *Star Wars*."

"The movie?"

"Precisely. They ran a simulation on what would happen if George Lucas has never been there to make *Star Wars*. In fact, it turned out to be a very useful model. Can you imagine the consequences if George Lucas was removed from the timeline?"

Miller laughed. "Well, for one thing we would have been spared Jar Jar Binks."

"Pardon?"

"A character from one of the awful *Star Wars* prequels. One of the worst movie characters ever."

"Okay. But it's much more than that. There would be no prequels or originals. There would be no *Star Wars* at all."

Miller thought about that. He'd miss the original trilogy, of course, but he couldn't see that its absence would have much of an impact beyond that. "Other than people having to come up with another nickname for Reagan's Space Defense Initiative, the only people this would hurt would be the buyers and sellers of all the *Star Wars* merchandise. And I suppose Mel Brooks wouldn't have made *Spaceballs*."

Price shifted into professorial mode in spite of himself. He was going to make Miller realize just how shortsighted he was being. "That's really all you see?"

"No *Star Wars*, no sequels, spinoffs, or ripoffs. What else is there to worry about?"

"How about no *E.T.*?"

Miller was confused. "What are you talking about? *E.T.* was by Steven Spielberg, not George Lucas."

"My nerds were very thorough, and they had a lot to back up their conclusions. If it wasn't for George Lucas, Spielberg's career would likely have ended with his 1979 flop *1941*. He might have churned out a few minor films, but no one would have trusted him with a major project like *E.T.*"

This was all before Miller was born, but he did know his pop culture, especially post-*Star Wars*. He looked at Price. "That's absurd. Spielberg had had a huge comeback with *Raiders of the Lost Ark*. He could write his own ticket after that came out."

"Check and mate," replied Price. "My nerds pointed out that *Raiders* would never have been made without Lucas. After the flop of *1941* Spielberg was at a loss, and he met up with his friend Lucas. They came up with the idea of *Raiders* and Lucas agreed to produce it. That's what got it made."

Miller wasn't convinced. "Spielberg might have come up with it on his own. Other directors have bounced back from flops."

"But who would star in it?"

"What do you mean? Why couldn't Harrison Ford play…" Miller stopped short.

"That's right. Without Lucas, Harrison Ford would have gone back to his career as a carpenter, having never gained traction in Hollywood. He never would have been in *American Graffiti* or *Star Wars*. He'd have been one of those young actors who got a few TV credits and then was never heard from again."

"Okay, if there was no Lucas, it would have impacted the careers of Ford and Spielberg."

Price shook his head. "You're still not seeing the bigger picture. If there was no George Lucas there would be no *Star Trek* revival, and I would have had nothing to show Alison."

"What are you talking about? Lucas had nothing to do with *Star Trek*."

"Actually, he did, in more ways than one. Let's start with the obvious. The *Star Trek* revival started in 1979 with the release of the first movie. The only reason it was made was because of the success of *Star Wars*."

"How do you know that?" Miller was getting annoyed. Price was starting to make sense. He was finding connections where there shouldn't have been any connections at all.

"Don't underestimate the power of nerds with access to Internet search engines. It turns out that in 1977, Paramount studios was actively planning to launch a fourth television network, several years before Rupert Murdoch started FOX."

"So, what does that have to do with *Star Trek?*" asked Miller, already anticipating that he wouldn't like the answer.

"The linchpin for the new network was going to be the launch of a new *Star Trek* series with nearly all of the original cast. Of course, the network didn't happen but the success of *Star Wars* convinced Paramount that a *Star Trek* movie could succeed as well. As a result of that, the first *Star Trek* movie was released in 1979, leading to a whole film series as well as several new television series."

Miller was flabbergasted. "I had no idea."

"And *Star Wars* did more than set off a science fiction boom in Hollywood. My grad students took it even further, and showed that the very nature of moviemaking would have been different."

The reporter knew he was beaten, but he had to see it through to the end. "How?" was all he could ask.

Price took pity on the reporter. "The success of *Star Wars* allowed Lucas to set up several different companies that focused on different aspects of the industry. Industrial Light & Magic was his special effects arm. It was not only involved in innovating new movie effects, but it became the go-to place for the entire film industry. Eventually, there would be rival companies, as well as others that would be formed by Lucas alumni, but looking at just Industrial Light & Magic in the 1980s, no fewer than forty different productions used them in whole or part for their special effects. And it wasn't just Lucas's own movies, nor was it only just science fiction movies like the *Star Trek* films. By the next decade, it would more than double to over one hundred different movies and other projects."

Miller knew when he was defeated. It took him a moment, but then he dredged up the appropriate response. "You see, George, you really had a wonderful life," he quoted.

"Pardon?"

"It's from an even older movie. *It's a Wonderful Life*. The angel, Clarence, tells George Bailey, 'Each man's life touches so many other lives.' I guess your nerds proved it."

Miller couldn't quite believe what he been put through since this morning. He wondered how much more there was to go. Price rose. "Let's head back to campus," the professor said. "We're nearing the end of the story. I don't know if I can finish it in the ride back, but I'll do my best."

The reporter rose after hitting "send" on the terse email message he had sent to his editor about coming in late tomorrow. Just let him try to object. Miller was considering putting in for combat pay. "Let me guess. Alison turns out to be George Lucas's mother."

Price chuckled. "Oh no, not quite. But the news we faced when we celebrated Thanksgiving that fall would prove to be quite dramatic enough."

JOLTS

It had been a wonderful summer. Henry had never installed air conditioning in the house and relied on fans, which he thought were sufficient. There were fans of all shapes and sizes placed in every room of the house. I convinced Alison that they were no solution to the summer heat for two reasons. First, all they did was move the hot air around. The slight benefit of assisting with the evaporation of sweat was insufficient to someone like myself, who had grown up with central air conditioning. It's not like central air was some exotic device from the far future. Its use dated back to at least the 1930s. Installing central air conditioning in the Gondelman house was not impossible, but it would have entailed a lot of expense and construction. I had a simpler solution. I purchased a 1978 air conditioner unit, and installed it in the master bedroom. This became our lair for most of the summer. We emerged for food and drink, sundry chores, and to dispose of Henry's trash (coming across a 1967 memo on snow emergency procedures really hurt when the thermometer was topping 95 degrees Fahrenheit). When one box was completed, there was always another to pull in and sort through.

Cooler weather returned with the arrival of autumn and the start of a new school year. I had spent the whole summer with Alison, making brief jumps home to 1998 each week to deal with my mail and any messages. Now we were back to our school-year schedule of Fridays to Sundays along with holidays. I was eagerly anticipating Thanksgiving, because we planned to spend nearly a whole week together. We had not gotten together the weekend just before in order to get our school responsibilities out of the way without any distractions. I suppose I could have brought back papers back with me to 1978 to grade, but there was always the risk of one of them being mislaid and turning up inconveniently, like before the student was actually born, or containing information that was clearly out of its time.

Packed in my bag was a bottle of a 12-year-old Lagavulin single malt I had splurged on. I have to admit that I was somewhat amused at the thought that we'd be drinking it eight years *before* it had been put in the cask. It would go well with our Thanksgiving feast. Although it would be just the two of us for the weekend, her concession to the lack of a more extensive guest list was that she would simply make less of everything. We would still have the full variety of dishes which would, presumably, provide us with plenty of leftovers.

I arrived at noon, expecting to find Alison in the kitchen getting organized. Instead, the only one there when I appeared was Spock. He gave a brief start and then, when he saw it was only me, went back to cleaning himself.

I went out into the living room. The TV was tuned to some newscast. Alison was on the couch, tears streaming down her face. It took me a moment to process what was going on, and then I dropped my bag and rushed to her side. I put my arm around her.

"Alison, what's the matter? Did someone die?"

She pointed to the television set. A sober looking news anchor looked out as if he couldn't quite believe the news himself, "...the murder of Congressman Leo Ryan and several journalists only deepens the mystery of the deaths of at least 400 members of the People's Temple in Guyana. While most of the victims appear to have been poisoned, there are reports that their leader, the Reverend Jim Jones, died of a gunshot wound. There are still hundreds of people unaccounted for, although those few survivors who have managed to escape and get rescued reported hearing gunfire from the surrounding jungle. We have some of the first pictures from the site, and we warn viewers that these are disturbing images that you may not wish to see. I have to warn you, there are veteran reporters here in our newsroom who found them shocking..." On the screen was a photograph of bodies neatly arranged in rows as if they were from some ghastly children's play set.

Alison looked at me through her reddened eyes. "You must have known this was going to happen. Why didn't you warn me?"

More images appeared on screen, but it was only when the news anchor talked about people drinking down cyanide-laced grape Kool-Aid that it all clicked. It was the Jonestown Massacre. The grape drink turned out not to be Kool-Aid, but that hardly mattered. It was one of the most horrific news stories of modern times. I had completely forgotten that the story had broken just before Thanksgiving that year.

I held her closer. "I'm so sorry. I didn't know, or at least I didn't remember. I was only eight when this happened, and my mother wanted to shield me from it." Indeed, I now recalled that our television set had mysteriously broken that week, and I had missed watching the Thanksgiving parade. It had only gotten "fixed" when I went back to school.

"How could something this evil be allowed to happen? This must be what the liberators of the death camps felt like when they first entered and found the survivors: overwhelmed by the human capacity for cruelty." I got up to turn the television set off, but Alison shouted, "No!"

"It's only upsetting you, and it's not like we can do anything from thousands of miles away." Of course I learned more about it as I got older, especially when there would be news reports around the tenth anniversary of the event. Then I remembered something else. "Alison, you really don't want to watch this. There are many more than 400 dead. They've only started to discover all the bodies."

"Leave the TV alone," she insisted, but she allowed me to take her out of the room into the kitchen.

I went back to the living room to get my bag and retrieve the scotch. Alison sat at the kitchen table, idly petting Spock, who had jumped in her lap and was purring loudly. Sometimes animals instinctively know their humans need comforting. I got out a couple of glasses and gave us two generous pours. This was not the time to ask her how she liked her scotch, or if she even drank scotch. She emptied half the glass in a single swallow. "I can add some water to that…"

"I don't understand how something like this could happen," she said, ignoring my offer. "And how could you not have remembered it?"

A second swallow on my part allowed me to catch up with her. "I was a child. My mother was very protective. I'm remembering now that there was some question whether we would be joining the family for Thanksgiving dinner."

"Why?"

"For the simple reason that—as I later learned—it was the number one topic around the table that year. It was all anyone could talk about. For the only time I can remember, the children's table was in another room."

It was a somber week. Alison had to follow the news. She claimed it was important for the book she hoped to write some day. We neglected Henry's boxes. They'd still be there next week. I let her watch as much of the news coverage as she could take, and then led her away when it got be too much. When they started discovering that the corpses that we had seen in the initial photos were, in fact, covering more bodies beneath them, those of children and even infants who had been given the evil brew of fruit drink, sedative, and cyanide, and then laid down to die, I had to leave the room. I could only be glad that we were not yet in the era of 24-hour cable news channels.

Thanksgiving dinner was scaled back. She had only planned to roast a turkey breast, not an entire bird, and she talked me through the process. I became her kitchen puppet, not quite knowing what I was doing, but following instructions at her direction. She took over the vegetables when my competency was not up to her exacting standards, and I was grateful the scotch made it to the end of the week.

The death toll topped 900, but by the weekend, Alison decided she had learned enough. Either that, or else she could later catch up on her own. After the 11 P.M. newscast on Friday, she turned off the television herself. We had the first moment of quiet since I had arrived on Tuesday afternoon. We had had some leftovers for dinner, and the plates were still on the coffee table in front of the couch in the living room.

"It can wait until morning," she said, taking my hand and leading me upstairs.

We made love quietly and intently, almost in a spirit of defiance. It was the first time since I had gotten there. In a week that had been all about death, this was a declaration affirming life. Afterwards, as I held her, I could feel some tears, but I said nothing. I knew her well enough by now. She had to work this through in her own way. I let her know I was there for her, when and how she needed me.

Finally she looked at me. "Tell me about the future, Willy, the marvelous, magical future where you can't keep track of all the new episodes of *Star Trek* and everyone has a personal computer and the Soviet Union has vanished and evil like this can't be allowed to happen."

I kissed her wet cheeks. "I'm sorry, Alison. We haven't solved the problem of evil. Terrible things still happen. There are still murders and wars and natural disasters…"

"But nothing like this, right Willy?"

I knew that wasn't the case. There was nothing like this involving *Americans*, but I knew that wasn't what she wanted to hear. "I don't live in Utopia, Alison. It's just different, that's all."

She looked at me. "All over America, families gathered for Thanksgiving dinner and they talked about mass murder occurring in some country which they probably couldn't have found on a map last week. If you had stayed home in 1998—if there was no time machine—what would you have been talking about?"

I had to think about that. I wasn't much of a news junkie, and between Alison and our ongoing review of Henry's papers, I barely had time to focus on my classes, much less anything else. Of course there was one story that was dominating the news. I didn't know how I would be able to tell her about it, since I barely understood it myself.

"I guess it would be the impending impeachment of the president."

She gasped. This was the most shocking thing she had heard all week that wasn't related to Jonestown. "You're kidding! Impeachment? We didn't even get that far with Nixon. What did he do? Divert government funds to a private bank account in Switzerland? Sell military secrets to a foreign power? Murder someone?"

How was I going to explain this? "As near as I can tell, he was messing around with an intern."

Alison did something I hadn't heard in a long while from her. She laughed. She laughed long and loud, and it was probably more than was required under the circumstances, but I think it was as much for the release as anything else. She had been grieving for days, and the admittedly absurd circumstances surrounding the impeachment of Bill Clinton certainly seemed amusing from a distance. When she finally recovered some modicum of self-control, she said, "I'm sorry. That's just so funny. For a moment I actually thought you said he was being impeached for messing around with an intern."

"I did. And lying about it."

She started laughing again. "Let me get this straight. The president diddled some intern and lied about it and *that's* why he's being impeached? Who's bringing the charges against him, his wife?"

"Um no, it's the special prosecutor."

This brought a new peal of laughter. "The special prosecutor? You mean like in Watergate? You have a special prosecutor just for adultery?"

"To tell you the truth, I don't understand it all myself. The Republicans keep saying it has nothing to do with sex, but as far as I can tell, it's all about the sex."

"This is the big news in 1998?"

"It's what people are talking about."

"It sounds like a very silly world," said Alison. She was quiet for a moment. "I'd much rather be talking about sex than about mass death."

"If it matters, the public opinion polls seem to show that people are taking the president's side. Not that they approve of his cheating, but they don't seem to think that this is any business of Congress."

Alison started laughing again. "And you're not making this up?"

I put up my hand. "I swear."

She kissed me again. "I love you, Willy. When we're done with Dad's papers, you've got to find a way to take me to your silly future. I think I could be very happy there with you."

We held each other close. As we drifted off to sleep, I wondered if bringing Alison to my time would ever be possible. I kept checking Henry's third notebook, but he had yet to offer me anything that suggested how it might be done.

Valentine's Day fell on a Wednesday in 1979, but we managed to arrange our schedules to be together. We both had to take some time off on Thursday—Alison for a class and me for office hours in 1999—but we felt we had earned it. I even had a surprise for her. I was never going to be a gourmet cook, but I had learned to make a simple dish involving salmon and white wine, and prepared it for us on Friday night. The rice and French cut green beans came out of the frozen food section, and I let her handle the salad and dessert, but the fish involved real cooking. It was real *simple* cooking, but it counted. I wanted to show her how much she meant to me, and how much of an impact she was having on my life. Alison very much appreciated it. Oddly, she showed her appreciation by talking about death and religion.

The dishes were loaded in the dishwasher and the leftovers put away in the fridge, and we were down to nibbling on some cheese and sipping a German *liebfraumilch*, a somewhat sweet white wine that was perfect for the end of a meal. I could tell she was bursting to tell me something, and since my week had consisted of preparing a midterm and failing to puzzle out a difficult passage in Henry's notebook, I had nothing much to offer.

"You liked the salmon?" I asked.

"It was wonderful. It melted in my mouth."

"That's all I needed to hear," I said. "I'm all yours. What have you been up to?"

She placed a slice of whatever cheese she had served on a cracker and took a bite. "I've had an insight that makes a lot of sense to me. I don't know if it will make sense to you, but let's see." She allowed herself a sip of wine. "Okay, let's start with the idea that every religion offers us some notion that our lives continue beyond our initial time on Earth. We go to heaven. We get reincarnated. We await resurrection on Judgment Day. The life force is somehow preserved."

"Okay," I replied. "I don't pretend to any great expertise in this area, but that certainly sounds a lot like what I've heard."

"No one knows for sure, of course, and there are those who say we only get one go-around and that's it. However, if Einstein was right, energy and matter can't be obliterated. One may turn into the other, but in the end, the universe preserves itself."

This is precisely why I had avoided taking philosophy classes in college. I poured myself the last of the wine. Alison was on a roll, and she certainly didn't need any more. "Okay," I offered, not feeling equipped to challenge her.

"So why should the energy of the life force be any different? Until now, we had no reason to suspect that life survives the way energy and matter does, but your device shows otherwise. We all die—that's a given —but we also live forever."

The wine bottle was empty, and I had brought no scotch this time, so I had no choice but to try to make sense of this. "How can we both die and live forever?" It wasn't exactly a Socratic dialogue, but it was all I had.

"You proved it yourself."

Now I was not only looking at the bottle being empty, I was looking at the label. Had I been drinking wood alcohol instead of wine? "You've lost me. How did I prove it?"

"We're used to thinking of time as sequential. It's one thing after another, always moving into the future. It's like being on a train, going from the starting terminal to the end of the line. You're always moving forward, and that's the whole point of the journey."

"And that's wrong?"

"Willy, let me ask you a question. You're here in America. Does that mean China doesn't exist?"

Wait, I could handle this one. "Of course not." Nailed it!

"Exactly. You're here in the 20th century. Does that mean the 18th century doesn't exist?"

"Well, it did exist once."

She smiled. "Listen to yourself. You're captive to your assumptions. Why are you treating time different from space?"

"Because it's in the past?"

"And when you went back to 1865, was it all in amber?"

I had to think about that for a moment. No, of course not. I had moved around freely. I had heard Lincoln speak. "No."

"And when you went to 1965, did you see your father frozen in a diorama?"

"No, I told you what happened."

"There you go," she said. "Time is like space. We may only perceive part of the universe, but it all exists whether we're seeing it or not. The same is true for time. We perceive 'now'—or whatever passes for 'now' to us—but that doesn't eradicate all of time. Your device lets us take our blinders off and see time as no more than another dimension. You can go into the past or see some part of the future. All of time exists at once, whether you can see it or not."

She was definitely her father's daughter. My head was throbbing. "I'm lost. If I'm going to die someday, why are you telling me I'm not?"

"Of course you're going to die someday. So am I. That's the fate of all us mortals. But we're also going to live forever. Anyone travelling through time to see us will find us just as we are. Just as you found my father. Just as you found me."

"But…"

"But what, dear Willy? It's not real? Am I not real? The past can't be changed? You've proven that wrong. You can't interact with the past? Then how come I know about *Star Trek* movies that have yet to be made? Don't you see? We live forever in the time in which we live. Just like China or India or Australia is there wherever you happen to be, so are all the times of history, whether you visit them—or *can* visit them—or not."

Something didn't strike me right about this. "What about God?" We'd never talked about religion, and I didn't know what her beliefs or non-beliefs were, but if one were to accept her view, it would seem to subvert a lot of deeply held beliefs held by *somebody*. Indeed, a lot of somebodies.

As it turned out, she had given this some thought at as well. "Does anyone know for sure that there is—or isn't—a God? And if there is, what God wants from us? We have ideas. We have different approaches and theories, but the bottom line is faith, not proof. No one *knows*. What your device does is settle one of the questions that have baffled theologians for millennia: the immortality of the soul. Do we have souls? I leave that to them. Do our souls or spirits or selves live for eternity? Yes, we do. If we ever existed in time, we exist for all time." She sat back with a satisfied smile.

"And what happens after we die?"

She gave me that semi-mocking look I'd come to know well. "How the hell should I know? You expect me to solve all of life's eternal mysteries in a single night?"

The end of the term came all too soon. I got my grades in and then headed back to 1979 to meet Alison. We had finally culled the Gondelman papers, reducing what had been over two hundred boxes down to twenty. We didn't worry about organizing them: it would be up to the library curators to catalog them in a way that made sense to future researchers. What concerned us were the two boxes that would be sealed for seventy-five years. One contained all sorts of personal information, like photographs and personal correspondence: all the things that no one had any real need to see except some far-off biographer, assuming that anyone would be interested in the life and times of Henry Gondelman in 2054. The other box contained the second notebook (I had my photocopies) and other odds and ends related to temporal mechanics that we decided to bury, because I felt it might give away too much too soon. We thought two out of twenty boxes marked "personal" and set aside for seventy-five years wouldn't call too much attention to themselves. There were plenty of papers to sift through, and holding back personal items until after the people mentioned were presumably long gone was not considered all that out of the ordinary for this kind of material.

I also learned—from reading over the agreement between Alison and the university—that the archivists were assuming what was called a "fiduciary duty." They were undertaking a positive obligation to keep those two boxes sealed, and could be sued by Alison (or her "heirs and assigns," whomever they might be) if they failed to do so. It seemed like a pretty safe deal.

I met her at "our" office as usual, and she greeted me by handing me a box full of books and pictures. "I'm glad you're here," she said. "I think we'll be able to get this to my car now in one trip."

"Hello to you too," I huffed, as much from annoyance as exertion. "Don't tell me you found more of your father's boxes?" We had cleared the office of his stuff more than a year ago.

"Sorry, Willy, I guess I'm just overexcited. This is all *my* stuff."

I put the box down on the desk. "Why are we moving your stuff?"

"Because I've quit. I was never cut out to be a physicist, and had no desire to go for my Ph.D. The only reason I pursued the Masters was to be able to get a teaching post here while I was sorting Dad's papers. And now we're done, and I can get on with my life." She picked up a box, and indicated I should take up mine. "I'll explain the rest on the drive home."

There wasn't much to explain. She had gotten a message from Henry —in writing, no personal contact—that he had set up a trust for her. The trust already owned the house, and now it would also see to it that she had a comfortable income deposited in a passbook savings account each month. This meant she no longer had to work or, more precisely, teach physics. She planned to devote herself to developing her "philosophy of temporal mechanics" and writing a book which might or might not be published in her lifetime. It also meant she could travel for indefinite periods and the house would be maintained, including having real estate taxes and other bills paid, with no one questioning where she was.

"Nice deal," I grunted, as I lugged one of the boxes from her car into the house.

I put it down in the foyer. She put its companion box next to it. "It's a very nice deal for both of us. Don't you see?"

"I'm afraid not."

"Willy, I'm free. I have nothing to tie me here. My father is my only living relative, and like Billy Pilgrim, he's become unstuck in time."

There were times I really had trouble following her. "Who's Billy Pilgrim?"

She rolled her eyes. Then she reached into one of her boxes and pulled out a book. "*Slaughterhouse-Five* by Kurt Vonnegut. You need to read this. In fact, given your own work, I'm amazed you haven't come across it by now."

I slipped the book into my bag. "What does any of that have to do with me, other than the fact that now you'll have a more flexible schedule?"

"There are times when you're incredibly sensitive and insightful. This isn't one of them," she said. "Willy, I can go with you. There's nothing holding me to this time any more. We can live here in the house in 1999. Our combined assets will mean neither of us has to work at anything we don't want to, although I assume you'll want to stay at the university and have access to all their resources and facilities." I must have still look dumbfounded, because she added, "Willy, it means we can together all the time in *your* time."

When I saw her frowning, I realized that I didn't appear enthused at the prospect, which wasn't the case at all. "Being with you would be wonderful. In fact, it *is* wonderful. I just don't know that the device can handle us and all your stuff traveling twenty years into the future."

"My stuff?"

"You know, your clothes, your personal belongings, your... oh, right." It had suddenly dawned on me if that the house was maintained for the twenty years of her absence, all her "stuff" would already be there in 1999.

"For someone who's such a genius, sometimes you can be really dense," she said, then softened the barb with a kiss. "Besides, the first thing I'll have to do once we get there is go shopping."

"Shopping? For what?"

"Follow me." We headed up to the bedroom, which seemed promising, even though I knew the university was coming up to pick up her father's boxes in half an hour. Instead of heading to the bed, she pulled open her closet doors. "To replace all of this."

I looked at her clothes and didn't understand what she was driving at. "Why? If you travel ahead twenty years, you'll still be the same size as you are now. They'll still fit."

She rolled her eyes. "So you think I'm going to get fat when I'm twenty years older? Thanks for the vote of confidence." I started to protest that that wasn't what I meant, but she stopped me. "Fashions change. If I dress like a '70s graduate student in 1999, I'm going to look like I came out of a time warp. I'll have to go out and buy a whole new wardrobe.

Perhaps I can use your computer to find out what women are wearing then, because it's obvious you're not going to be much help."

"I'm sorry. Clothes have never mattered all that much to me."

"Well, we'll work on that, too. In the meantime, it's quarter of one, and they're supposed to be picking up Dad's boxes at one. Help me put *my* boxes away, and then skedaddle. We'll talk more later."

We went back downstairs to fetch the boxes, first having to convince Spock they were not filled with cat toys. After they were stowed away, we exchanged the first proper hug of the day. I didn't want to let go, but we heard the university truck pull up in the driveway. An assistant librarian had arrived with a couple of workmen to cart away the boxes that were neatly stacked in the living room.

"I'll be back for dinner," I promised, and then pressed the button on the device in my bag, returning me to 1999. My departure removed the need for any explanations as to who I was and what I was doing at Alison's house in the middle of the afternoon. It also allowed me to perform my end of checking up on the transfer. All that stuff about "fiduciary duty" was fine, but I was in the unique position of being able to do a spot check twenty years later.

I looked around my office, and it seemed a bit different. Nothing had changed except for my sudden awareness that between Alison's departure in 1979 and my arrival here in the mid-1990s, someone else had been using the office. I had come to think of my office as a legacy from Henry and Alison. Well, there was no time to think about that right now. I headed off to the library. I had work to do.

I was a bit self-conscious as I passed through the detectors inside the front entrance. There was no question that I was in my proper place in Time, but I glanced around to see if anyone would try to challenge me. No one did. I rode the elevators to the offices on the fourth floor, and headed to the university archives. I asked the person at the desk if I might examine the file on Henry Gondelman. The boxes themselves were all in storage in some warehouse facility several miles from the campus. If I wanted to see them, I'd have to fill out an official request and wait for them to be transported to the main campus. A member of the faculty exploring the library's archives with regard to a prominent member of his department from the past might not be an everyday occurrence, but it was —fortunately—not so unusual that it drew any suspicion.

When the file was retrieved and turned over to me, I saw that the folder was a very slim one, containing of only a few typed pages. On the first sheet was a breakdown of the archive's holdings. There were the eighteen boxes that I had helped pack, with detailed lists of what each contained. Some material had been shifted from one box to another, but that was none of my concern. Then there were two boxes "sealed until May 15, 2054." That was precisely as I had previously found them, when I had made my foray into the archives two years ago. Then, to my surprise and delight, was a sheet containing a list of all the requests for access to the material. It turned out that only two people had come to the library to see Henry's papers. There was an author who had been here in 1985 and who had spent a few days rummaging through the public boxes. I recognized the name. He had written a book entitled *The Mystery of Henry Gondelman*, in which he not only explored an extremely crude understanding of temporal mechanics—mostly an oversimplification of what had been in Henry's 1972 book about sub-atomic particles—but also suggested that Henry's disappearance was evidence of a larger conspiracy which involved both the CIA and the space aliens who had reportedly landed in Roswell, New Mexico, in 1947. I was sorry Henry had to suffer this indignity, but he had no one to blame but himself for pulling his disappearing act. Fortunately, the book had similarly vanished.

What was interesting was that in 1997 someone had apparently tried to access the two sealed boxes. They couldn't do it physically, of course, but they had put in the request, and there was a memo from some member of the library staff that the person, who was unidentified, felt there was vital information contained therein which needed to be immediately accessed. The request was denied as a matter of course, and there was no further notation of any further action or interest. I ran through the file one more time, just to make sure I had not missed anything, and then returned it to the staff member.

"No need to request anything today. Nice to know it's there if I should need it. Thank you."

I left knowing that my request to see the file would *not* be recorded, just as my visit two years ago hadn't been, since I had not sought to examine any of the material. As of 1999, I could assure Alison, the material was being handled just as had been requested.

Before I headed back to Alison in 1979, it was time to confront the issue I had been dodging for some time: her "moving" to 1999. Did I want to be with her? Absolutely. Over the last two years and more, it had become clear that we were meant for each other. We complemented each other in so many ways that it almost felt like we were adjoining pieces in a jigsaw puzzle. We also had an easy compatibility when it came to our approaches towards life and what we wanted out of it, particularly in trying to figure out what it meant to lead a meaningful one. Our approaches might be different, but we were asking the same questions, and our individual answers seemed to feed each other. So what was the problem?

Quite simply it was the tech. I didn't think the device could take us both twenty years into the future without a serious malfunction, and I had no idea what that might mean. Except for Henry's disappearance and my one day jump with Alison nearly three years ago—well, twenty-three years ago, from the perspective of 1999—the only direct observation I'd had of time travel was my own experience, which could hardly be held to be conclusive. I didn't know how solve this. Henry, as it turned out, had his own ideas.

I came back to my office from the library to see the third notebook on my desk. There was no doubt what it was. The other two notebooks were now part of the Henry Gondelman collection at the library. I had no idea how he knew I would need his advice right now. Someday I would make him tell me. It would presumably be after I finished beating him over the head with his own book for what he was putting me and his daughter through with his cloak and dagger messages and mysterious ways.

> *Willy* (he wrote, somewhat informally, I thought),
> *Use Device 1.1.*
> *Henry*

Really? That's all he had to say, after months and months of silence? Alison got a trust fund from his last appearance. At the very least, I thought I might get an explanation as to what he was up to, but no, it was just enough to push me along.

It was the answer to my dilemma, of course. The device my future self had brought me was safely put away so that I could uphold the other end of the transaction when it was my time in the future to give it to him. The version I was using now—Device 2.0—was the one with the GPS/sonar improvement that Henry's own calculations had suggested. In between was the duplicate of the original that I had constructed to avoid damaging the one I'd have to give my younger self someday. It had worked just fine, and there was no reason Alison couldn't use that while we traveled forward together. Since clothes and "stuff" wasn't an issue, it should do the trick. I removed it from the locked box within the equally locked cabinet in my office (no use taking unnecessary chances) and placed it in my bag.

It was late afternoon now, and Alison would be expecting me at 5 P.M. in her time. Since I could leave for her time whenever I felt like it, I took a moment to sit and think. I allowed myself a small pour, and contemplated the action I was about to take. I loved Alison. There was no question. Did I want to share the rest of my life with her? Of course I did. Would she be able to fit into the world after a twenty-year jump? Well, no doubt there would be a lot for her to learn, but she'd already made the biggest leap in accepting that such a thing was even possible. I drained the glass and made my decision. With my eyes wide open, I went back to 1979 to bring the woman I loved home.

The pickup had gone off without a hitch, but I already knew that from my time in the library. I asked Alison if she wanted to go anywhere, perhaps out to a favorite restaurant, to say farewell to 1979. No. To the contrary, she wanted to wait until we arrived in 1999, and then go someplace that would seem exotic to her. She couldn't wait to dive into the future.

We had decided to make the move early on Saturday morning. I don't recall who came up with the idea, but its romanticism appealed to me. We would head down to the river where we had had our first lunch together, and sit on the same bench and watch the sun rise. As the new day dawned, we would make the jump.

We turned in early that night. The alarm was set for 4 A.M., giving us plenty of time to pull ourselves together and get to the river. There was a last-minute holdup when she pulled out the cat carrier. I hadn't thought of

Spock at all, but she had. We couldn't leave him behind. Even with the house being tended to, that didn't mean someone would come to feed him and give him fresh water and change his litter box every day. Even if such arrangements were possible, there was no way the seven-year-old cat was likely to survive another twenty years. It would have been just plain cruel to leave him on his own, alone in the house. Alison might have given him away, but she had no close local friends, and placing him in the local shelter was a crap shoot. He might get adopted, but more likely it would be a death sentence. It looked like I was not only bringing my girlfriend into the future, but her cat as well. I hope they hadn't changed the recipe of "Mixed Grill."

Alison convinced me of the logic of this being the right thing to do in just under two minutes. Unfortunately, she did not speak "cat," so it took another forty minutes to get Spock into the pet carrier. Finally, amidst much protesting, he was locked inside and ready to travel. The eastern sky was just starting to lighten as we made our way to the bench. I had my briefcase in my lap, and she had the pet carrier in hers. I pulled out the two devices. I set them both for the same location precisely twenty years in the future.

"You'll probably notice a slight jump," I explained. "The sunrise won't be precisely synchronized, but it should be close enough."

She took the backup device and placed it atop the carrier. "As long as I'm with you, it will always be enough."

"I love you, Alison Gondelman."

"I love you, Willy Price."

As the sun began to creep over the horizon she began to count down. "10... 9... 8..."

"What are you doing?"

"I'm counting down. This is a historic experiment." When I looked at her blankly, she said, "It's the first time two devices have operated in tandem. Where's your sense of drama?"

I smiled, and joined her in the countdown. "7... 6... 5... 4... 3... 2... 1... Go!"

We pressed the buttons on our devices together. I closed my eyes, knowing that when I opened them, the next chapter of our lives would be about to begin.

When I opened them, I was entirely alone.

THE HOME STRETCH

Price paid off the cab driver and joined Miller on the steps of the academic quad. It was just before 11 P.M. on a weeknight, and most of the students were back in the dorms. The few stragglers still out at this hour were too focused on their own agendas—feeding a case of the munchies from the sub truck, or hurrying off to overnight obligations at the campus radio station or newspaper—to notice the two men.

The professor took Miller's hand. "Max, I want to thank you for listening to me ramble on all day. I'm sure you want to get home now. " He shook the reporter's hand and started to head off.

"What?" shouted Miller, loud enough that a couple of students heading to the student union turned to look from the other end of the quad. Miller caught himself and lowered his voice. "Are you kidding? You can't just run off now."

"I don't understand. You made it clear you were indulging me. I appreciate it, really I do. I hope that dinner tonight made up for the amount of time you lost, given that I haven't given you anything to write about for the newspaper." Price's face was utterly bland, as if he was thanking a grad student who had dropped off the assignment he had been tasked with grading.

"Willy, you can't stop now. This is a cliffhanger. I've got to know what happened next. Were you able to find her?"

Price kept the same expression a few more beats, and then laughed. "Of course I'll tell you what happened. We're nearing the end of the story. I just wanted to see if I finally learned how to maintain a poker face. Thanks for confirming it." The professor was still chuckling as he led Miller to a bench a little ways down a path towards the business school.

The reporter was wondering once again if Price had all his marbles, but at this point he had to see it through. There was just no way he would willingly go home without hearing the end of this story, even if he didn't believe a word of it. "You know, you're pretty strange, Willy, and I've got to tell you, I had some truly eccentric professors when I was an undergraduate here. Those guys were like a buttoned-down Wall Street law firm compared to you."

He patted the reporter on the knee. "Lighten up, Max. You'll live longer."

The moon came out from behind a cloud. It was a classic Hunter's Moon lighting up the autumn evening. There was a hint of winter to come in the air, but only a hint. It was actually a mild October evening, and nothing was going to prevent Miller from hearing the end of the story. "Okay, Willy, I'm all ears. What happened next?"

Price's tone changed as he shifted back to his story. "What happened? I was devastated."

"If I can, let me take you through this step by step. First, you were alone?"

"That's right," replied Price somberly. "One moment I was with the woman who meant everything in the world to me—and her cat—and the next moment it was just me."

"And *you* were back home in 1999?"

The professor sighed at the memory. "Yes, Max, I was home. Home alone. The first thing I did was check my device to make sure it had worked. It was in perfect operating order. It had worked the same as it always had. If I had any doubts, they were quickly brushed aside when I saw my cell phone was reconnected to the network again."

"So what happened to Alison?"

"That's the question, isn't it? It would be the central question of my life for a long time to come."

Miller was engaged now and in full reporter mode. His feelings could be put away until later. For the moment, his goal was to elicit the full story from Price. The fact that he didn't believe any of it was almost beside the point. As a journalist, he was used to being lied to. He followed a basic process: first get the quote; he could always check the facts later.

"What did you do?"

"The first thing I did was go back to 1979, to see if something had gone wrong with her device. And that's when I was discovered that I was locked out."

It took a moment for Miller to process this. Then he gasped. "You were blocked from going back to that moment?"

Price, who had been so jovial only a few minutes before, now seemed devastated as he recalled the memory. "Not just that moment when we were getting ready to leap into the future. I was locked out of my entire time with Alison. I could not access anything from the moment I first met her to the moment we were on that bench with Spock."

"Were you blocked from the timeframe completely, or only from the environs of the university and her house?"

Price favored the reporter with a smile. "Excellent question. You're grasping what the quandary was. It took me quite a number of futile attempts before I came up with the idea to try to go back to that time in another location."

Miller got a certain satisfaction at this, but he could preen later. "And what happened then?"

"I adjusted the spatial coordinates. I was able to go back to 1979 to about 100 miles away, but no closer. Once I realized this would work, I went back to 1999 and loaded my pockets up with change, then I returned to 1979 earlier in the day. I tried calling Alison. I got a recording telling me 'all circuits were busy.' I made numerous attempts from various locations at different times. It didn't matter. I would not be permitted to get through."

"Why?"

"There was no way of knowing why Time would not allow me to contact her, considering this was during a period when we were practically living together. It was a paradox, to be sure, but there was no one for me to turn to for advice."

They sat quietly on the bench for a bit. They could hear the tolling of the hour from the library bell tower. Since it was 11 P.M., it took several moments. Finally, the ringing stopped, and Miller asked, "Was Henry able to offer you any help?"

The professor smiled again. "For someone who doesn't believe a word I've said, you've certainly got a good grasp of the details."

Miller kept his focus. "Well, did he try to contact you?"

"Yes. It was Saturday afternoon. At that point, I was more frustrated than I'd ever been in my life. After having spent several futile hours trying to go back to find Alison, I went to my office to see if there was anything from Henry. It was at that moment that I began to see why he chose to communicate via the notebook."

"Why was that?"

"Because if he had delivered his message in person, I think I would have killed him on the spot. The notebook was out on my desk. I spotted it as soon as I entered the office. I rushed over to it, hoping against hope there'd be some information I could actually use."

"And what was there?" asked Miller quietly.

"This is the hard part. Have faith."

"That's it?"

"That was it. Not even a 'Dear Willy' or 'Alison is okay.' I suppose it would have been too much to ask for a course of action, considering that her using the backup device had been his suggestion in the first place."

"What did you do then?"

"I was drained," said Price. "I had spent hours trying to get back to the late 1970s, first to see Alison and, when that didn't work, to try to call her. This was the last straw. I wasn't able to think of what I should do next. Instead, I went home and collapsed. I ended up losing track of time for several days. I couldn't tell you if I ate, showered, or slept. One morning I woke up and decided that I had engaged in enough self-pity, and it was time to figure out what I was going to do now."

Miller asked, "So, what did you do? You seem to have been stymied at every turn."

Price sighed. "The first thing I did was turn on my computer to see what the date was. It was Thursday."

"You'd been out of it for days," said Miller, as much for confirmation that it was only days and not weeks as to prod him along with his narrative.

"Yes. It was in midmorning. I showered, shaved, put on fresh clothes, and sat down to try to think this through logically. I had tried to go back to her time. That didn't work. I had tried to get advice from Henry. That didn't work. The one obvious thing I hadn't done was to go to her house."

Miller perked up. "Of course. It was being held in trust for her."

The professor looked rueful. "I was hesitant. I had no idea what I'd find there. Suppose something went wrong with the backup device. I jumped ahead to 1999, while she was stuck in 1979. I had no way to go back to her, communicate with her, or otherwise rectify the situation. What if she thought I had abandoned her? I might be showing up to confront an Alison in her late forties, convinced that I had abandoned her.

And what if she wasn't bitter and vindictive? Suppose she had never stopped loving me? She would be nearly fifty while I was twenty-nine. Would I still love her then? *Could* I still love her? I didn't know. And if I showed up after an absence of twenty years, not having aged a day, and rejected her, what would she do? Would she kill herself? Would she kill me? Would she go mad?"

The reporter expelled the breath he hadn't realized he had been holding. "You were taking a big chance. You had no idea what to expect."

"You have no idea. As I began to consider all the scenarios, I froze. If Alison had been there, she could have helped me clarify my thinking, but of course if she had been there, I wouldn't have had to think through the problem. What would you have done?"

Miller considered Price's dilemma for a long time. Other than distant traffic sounds, the night was utterly quiet. Finally he broke the silence. "I would go. I'd have to go. However horrible the possible outcome might be, the agony of not knowing would be even worse."

The professor offered his grim smile again. "That was the same conclusion I came to myself. So early Friday afternoon, I headed over to Woodbine Avenue. The house was just as I remembered it. The paint was a bit more weather beaten, but the lawn and flowers were obviously being maintained. I parked my car in the street and headed up to the front door. You'll be surprised to learn I never rang the doorbell."

Miller was goggle eyed. "Why not?"

"I looked at the name over the bell. It wasn't 'Gondelman.' It was 'Cerier'."

The reporter gave him an odd look. "I don't understand."

"It could only mean one of two things. Either Alison had married someone else, and didn't need an inconvenient, 29-year-old lover out of her past showing up on her doorstep."

"Or…?"

Price sighed again. "Or, that she had vanished for good, and the house had either been rented out or sold outright."

"And then what happened?" asked Miller, not even knowing if was conducting an interview any longer, or simply couldn't bear the suspense of not knowing what came next.

"Then?" replied Price. "Then the hard part began."

THE HARD PART

I hated taking time away from my search for Alison, but time continued to proceed. I had classes to teach in the fall, and lectures to prepare. For the moment, I was stymied. I didn't know what I could do that I hadn't already done. So I did the only thing I could think of, which was to focus on my copy of Henry's second notebook. I devoted myself to improving the device in hopes that—somehow—it would lead to some breakthrough that would lead me to Alison.

Months turned into years. People wondered why I had never married and rarely socialized. My appearances at department and university events, which were occasionally required, could be measured in minutes. When, in 2005, an anonymous benefactor had endowed my chair in physics, I had no choice but to attend the department celebration.

There was a dinner in my honor that was the longest I had been away from my work in ages. The whole physics department was there, of course, as were several college officials. The university president made an appearance during the meal to read a statement praising me for my work in a field which was not specified. I couldn't be sure if it was because the new president—a former sociology professor—didn't have the vaguest notion of what I did, or because neither did anyone else in the department. All anyone knew was that a major bequest had been given to the university with the proviso that it be used in part to support the "Henry Gondelman Chair in Physics," and that I would be the first person to be so subsidized. I already had tenure, and now I had a lifetime sinecure, as another condition of the endowment exempted me from any university retirement requirements.

We were in a private room at some Japanese steakhouse near the campus. Some of the grad students who were included in the celebration were enjoying the show the chef was putting on at the table, arguing about the vectors and velocity involved in his flashing spatula and spinning knives. I think it was the sake talking. For my part, I was simply watching the clock and wondering when I would be allowed to leave. During the dessert course, Dr. Surkis came over and took the seat next to me. People had been coming and going from the seats next to me all evening, as they came to realize what an appalling dinner partner I was.

"Willy," she began quietly, "The whole department is proud of you. I'm proud of you. The donation will not only support you, but the work of several other faculty members."

"Happy to be of service," I replied, tipping my small china sake cup at her, and taking a sip. It was empty. I moved to refill it, but the small bottle was empty as well. I signaled the waitress I'd like another.

"It's none of my business," she continued, "but I'm concerned about you."

"Is there some problem with my work?" I asked, hoping to shut down this conversation as quickly as possible.

"No, none at all. You deliver your lectures. The students give you high marks in the evaluations. You get your grades in on time. There's been a bit of grumbling about your lack of publishing any new research, but the bequest has ended any complaints. You're pulling your weight."

"Then I guess everything's fine." The waitress came over with the hot sake. I ignored the burning of my fingers as I poured myself a fresh cup. Before I could raise it, Dr. Surkis put her hand on my wrist.

"Willy, you may be fooling the world, but you're not fooling me. I can't remember the last time I saw you smile. You have no social life that anyone is aware of. Students wonder if you're gay, or if you use the summers to take illegal sex tours in Asia."

"You're right," I said.

"Yes?"

"It's none of your business."

She stood. "Willy, I'm not trying to pry, but I want you to know I care. You can come and talk to me at any time. Or I can quietly and discreetly refer you to someone. It's not all on you."

I felt a little twinge. I had once said that to Alison, about sharing responsibilities. A thought suddenly occurred to me. "I appreciate it, Dr. Surkis. Perhaps there is something you can do for me."

"Name it. If it's in my power, it's yours."

"Didn't Henry Gondelman have a daughter who taught here?"

Dr. Surkis furrowed her brow. "Now that you mention it, yes. She taught for a few years in the late '70s. Why do you ask?"

"Oh, no reason," I said, casually. "I was just wondering if you had any contact information for her. I had some questions about her father's work."

She smiled. She seemed almost relieved. "No, we don't maintain an address list of past faculty, particularly the various adjuncts who pass through. They come and they go."

"Oh," I replied. It had been worth a shot.

"That's not to say I can't point you in the right direction."

I looked up, trying not to let my eagerness show. I wanted to scream at her to give me the information at once. Instead I said, "Really? How?"

"If I recall, she did some of her graduate work here. If anyone would know how to get in touch with her, the alumni office would. They'd track people down to desert islands if they thought it would lead to a donation."

"Yes, of course," I nearly shouted. People at other tables stopped what they were doing and looked at us. "Why didn't I think of that?" I leaned over and gave Dr. Surkis a big kiss on the cheek. "Thank you."

She was too stunned to react. Or if she did react, I was already out of the restaurant by the time she did. It was late Saturday night, and Monday was a holiday. The alumni office wouldn't open again until Tuesday. That would have been excruciating for most people. Of course, most people didn't have a time travel device. I had to get back to campus and power up my newly tweaked Device 3.0. It was essentially an upgrade on the GPS technology, providing me with a map of my destination. I set it for just outside the building where the Alumni Office was located. Tuesday morning was only a few minutes away.

As it turned out, the alumni office wasn't much use at all. After seeing that I was a prominent faculty member who was simply trying to track down a colleague in my field, they agreed to look up her address. It turned out to be the house on Woodbine Avenue.

"Nothing else?"

The twenty-something staffer, who wouldn't even have been born when Alison was here, shook her head. "It's not surprising, Professor Price. Graduate students don't always have the same ties to their schools that undergraduates develop. Have you checked where she went to college?"

If Alison had told me where she went to school before she came here, I didn't remember. "No, I don't know where she got her bachelor's degree. All I know is that it was somewhere in Ohio."

"I've got it right here. Would you like me to contact them to see if they have any newer information?"

"Would you?"

"Not a problem," she said with a smile. "Alumni offices don't always share that information with each other, since we're really development offices, and a donation to one school might mean the lack of a donation to another. Usually, though, they're willing to extend professional courtesy. Let me see what I can do. Can I have your number?"

I wrote done the number for my office, and she promised to get back to me as soon as she heard anything. My elation didn't last very long. I crossed the campus from the alumni office back to mine, and there was already a message waiting for me. They had the same address. Another dead end.

I was pretty certain that Alison couldn't be in my time anyway, because if she was, she certainly knew how to find me. Since I had heard nothing from her, I could only assume she was lost in time or worse. I paid work study students to search databases all over the internet, looking for any mention of her. There was nothing past 1979, and nothing much in the years prior.

As the years went by with no news, my mood got bleaker. I started to imagine that she was somewhere wondering why I had abandoned her, and perhaps even hating me for it. I felt so helpless. I did the only thing I could do: I redoubled my efforts to improve the Device.

Device 4.0 came about from some musings by Henry near the end of his notes about not only sending out signals ahead to determine if the space to be travelled to was already occupied or even existed, but a way to see if the time was open as well. When I was ready to test it, I attempted to travel back to 1979. Alas, the improvements worked precisely as I had designed them. I was informed that that time was closed to me. It couldn't say why, but that was only because I didn't know why myself, and couldn't program it to offer reasons. I kept moving back in time: November 1978, and that horrible Thanksgiving. No dice. August 1978, when she took me out to a new movie about college life that had just opened called *Animal House*. I didn't really know who John Belushi was, but she did—he had appeared on campus the year before, and was apparently a big comedy star of the era—and we had had a wonderful time. Nope, that was closed off as well. I went all the way back to September 1977, when we had first met. Still closed. On a whim, I tried September 1976. The green light went on. I could go back to September 1976! I could find Alison.

I pressed the Go button without thinking. I appeared in her/my office, but fortunately it was noontime, and no one was there. I quickly slipped out of the office, down the stairs, and out of the building. All right, it was September 1976. I had no idea if she was on campus today or not. I probably should have done a bit of research first to see if I could find her teaching schedule, but I had carried this ache within me for so many years that I just couldn't wait.

It was a beautiful, late summer day. If she was here today and having lunch around now, perhaps she'd be down by the river. I crossed the quad, avoiding some dog playing catch with two boys tossing a Frisbee, and headed through the visitor's parking area. From there, it was just a matter of crossing the street.

I followed the path along the river for a ways, and then I saw her. I stopped and choked up. There she was, in the same spot where she'd be sitting when I would last see her two and a half years from now. I wanted to run toward her and take her in my arms and never let go. And, just as I was ready to be reunited with my lost love, I suddenly realized I had made a horrible mistake.

Not only was this the year before we had met, so she did not yet know me except, perhaps, as a name mentioned by her father. She was also a year younger than when we had first met, making her around 24. Meanwhile I was now in my early forties. If I walked up to her and professed my love, she wouldn't see me as the man she would someday love. She would see this creepy old guy who was coming on to her. That is, if she didn't start laughing at how pathetic I must look.

I continued along the path, walking by the bench, trying not to stare. She was as lovely as I remembered, reading a book as she ate her lunch. I glanced at the cover. It was *Slaughterhouse-Five*, the book she had given me. It was probably that very book. My eyes welled up with tears, and I kept walking. My heart was pounding, and I was wondering if I was going to have a heart attack. At least if I were to die now, I would have seen her one more time. I couldn't take it any longer. I pressed the button to return to the present.

Several more years went by. Whenever the phone rang or there was a knock on the door, I hoped for a fleeting moment it might be Alison. Maybe her device had caused her to overshoot 1999, and she ended up several years later, and had found me at last. Alas, it never was.

I continued to walk through my life while barely participating in it. When required, I got up just enough energy to do whatever it was I needed to do. I was fortunate in that I was able to compartmentalize. For the hour or so I was in front of a classroom, the rest of my life disappeared. I could be the honored professor giving a lecture, asking and answering questions, and making sure that I was doing my job. Grading exams and papers were chores largely shunted off to my teaching assistants—rank has its privileges—and I made sure to buy them all nice but not overly ostentatious gifts at the end of semester. I didn't want anyone to claim I was overcompensating for the fact that I barely talked to any of them during the term.

Dr. Surkis stopped making me go to department events, although once or twice each semester she would make a point of trying to engage me in conversation. It rarely lasted more than a minute or two. What could she do? I was doing my work. I didn't seem to be harming myself or anyone else. What I asked in return was to be left alone. There was one more improvement for the device that Henry foresaw, and that's what I devoted myself to whenever I could. It would provide a memory bank of all the places and times the device had previously been to, which would not only provide a useful record, but be of assistance if one needed to return to exactly the same moment. It was not as easy as it appeared, but I thought I might be close to testing out the prototype for this final tweak.

When I was approaching my 50th birthday, I started getting solicitations for retirement funds and to join groups devoted to senior citizens and the like. I considered myself still young, with many productive years ahead of me and, as with most of the mail that I received, such material was quickly diverted to the trash. One day one such letter caught my eye. In large print, it told me all about the tax advantages of putting my assets into a trust and living off of the income. I was just about to toss it away with the rest of the day's mail when it jogged something in my memory. Henry had set up a trust for Alison to take care of the house and in order to provide her with a steady income. According to the letter, the law firm offering to set up a trust for me would fulfill their fiduciary obligations as trustees of my wealth, providing for me during my lifetime, and then for my hypothetical heirs after I was gone. I ignored most of this, and focused on something I should have picked up on a long time ago. If there's a trust, there has to be a trustee. Why hadn't I thought of this earlier?

If I could find the trustee who was maintaining Alison's house and other assets, I might be able to find out if he or she had heard from Alison, or whether they knew if she had been accessing any of the money in her savings account which, by now, must be quite considerable. So all I had to do now was call the trustee and ask...

My excitement came to a screeching halt. I had no idea who the trustee was, or even if it was a local law firm or some other institution. I didn't even know how to begin to look. I was stuck again, and so I returned to my usual gloom.

The following morning found me puzzling over the last few pages of Henry's notes and wondering why I hadn't received any message from him in years. I felt like one of those Biblical figures who heard from God for a little while and then no more. Henry was no god, of course, but at this point in my life, he was as mysterious and inaccessible as one. I realized I had no one to whom I could turn. At that moment, fate stepped in. Dr. Surkis's sympathetic attempts to reach me occurred randomly throughout the school year, without rhyme or reason. Perhaps it was only a matter of Time, or good timing, that she arrived at precisely the right moment.

"Willy, do you have a minute?" she asked, stepping into my office. She had long since stopped asking me to come to her office. To her amazement I greeted her with a smile.

"Why, yes. What can I do for you?"

She took the seat next to my desk and said this was probably the last time she would be bothering me, as she was finally retiring at the end of the semester. She had had a long run, and I would become someone else's problem. Until then, I was still hers. She wanted to know if I could make myself presentable for a potential donor who would be visiting the school next week. For some reason, I was one of the sights on the tour of the Physics Department, and I considered it part of my job to perform on command in such circumstances, not unlike a trained monkey. I agreed so quickly she seemed startled. Apparently, she thought she would have to cajole me into it. Of course I had been growing crankier with time, but now I had a new glimmer of hope.

"Do you know much about trusts?" I asked, trying to keep my voice as casual as possible.

"Not really," she answered. "What do you need to know?"

"Well, there's a house I'm interested in buying, but it's owned by some trust, and I have no idea how to figure out who or where they are."

"Well, that should be easy enough. You have to check the county land records. They're all online. It shouldn't be too complicated to find the name of the current owner."

I lit up with delight. I think I may have frightened her, because Dr. Surkis got up and moved quickly to the door. "Thank you," I told her.

"You're welcome. I'll be in touch about next week," she said, as she slid through the opening and closed it behind her. No doubt this would be recorded as another of those "crazy moments with Willy" that my colleagues collected. No matter. I had work to do.

I went online and quickly realized I had no idea where to start. I began by doing a web search for the local land records. I was directed to the website for the clerk's office for the county government. Land records going as far back as the 1970s were online, but I couldn't just call them up. In order to access them, I would first have to register with the website. The Internet was supposed to make life easier and our access to information faster. Instead, everyone wanted a "username" and a "password," and heaven forbid if it didn't like either. "Willy" was already taken, so I ended up registering as "WPrice." That seemed to be okay. Now I would need a password. The password had to have capital letters, small letters, numbers, a punctuation mark, and be at least fifteen characters long. It took me three tries to come up with the correct combination. I really didn't care. It wasn't like I'd be using this website again.

I thought now at last I could start my search, but there was one more hoop to jump through. To "confirm" my registration, they had sent me an email that would only be good for twenty-four hours. I had to retrieve the e-mail and click on the link contained therein. One would think I was trying to access the launch codes for the Strategic Air Command. I found the email and, with the link clicked, I now went back to the country clerk's website where, naturally, I had to log in. It took me four tries to remember the password I had just created. (I kept using the ";" instead of the ":".) At last I was in.

Now I had to figure out how to find the information I needed. I'm a distinguished professor of physics with an endowed chair, I thought. This shouldn't be too difficult. Ten minutes later—and several tries—I finally stumbled onto the correct listings. Looking up "declaration of trust" wasn't helpful, because I didn't know exactly when the trust had been created. Fortunately, the County Clerk's page was a bit more user friendly than the registration process. I realized that the most direct route to the information I wanted was to look up the records for who owned the house on Woodbine Avenue. I plugged in the address and there it was: it had been transferred in 1971 from Henry Gondelman to the Alison Gondelman Trust. No further transaction had taken place. The trust still held the property. There were further links that had to do with taxes and some such, and when I clicked on those, I found a receipt for the most recent real estate tax payment, which had been sent to the law firm of Marx & McCormick. A downtown address was provided. I printed out the receipt and logged off the site.

Finding the phone number of the firm was easily done. I called and asked to speak to the trustee for the Alison Gondelman Trust. The receptionist had no idea what I was talking about, but I was turned over to the secretary for one of the partners, who said that the person I needed to speak to was a Ms. Chang, who could see me at 5 P.M., if that was convenient.

"I can be there at 4," I said, ready to drop everything to see if this might lead me to finding Alison.

"In that case, you should bring something to read," replied the secretary tartly, "Ms. Chang will not be available until 5."

As it was, I got there at 4:30, and the attorney's conference call ran until 5:20. I could have cut the waiting time by jumping ahead with the device, but I didn't know precisely when she would be ready, and I didn't want to risk missing her. Finally, I was summoned and led past the reception desk down a quiet hallway. Most of the secretaries had left at 5, but some of the attorneys were still in their offices returning calls or reviewing documents. I was taken into a nicely decorated space without much of a view. I could see the office building across the street. I imagined that there probably weren't going to be any really good views from the fourth floor.

Still, there were some tasteful prints hung on the wall, along with a law school diploma, and some pictures on her desk of some children, presumably belonging to Ms. Chang. She rose from her desk and came around to greet me. As with everything else in the office, her clothes spoke of seriousness, taste, and savvy. I could only imagine how the rumpled academic I had become appeared to her.

"Professor Price," she said, extending her hand, "Please have a seat. Can I get you anything? Coffee? Water?"

I took the seat opposite the desk after waving off the offer of refreshments. "No, thank you."

She resumed her seat. "It's not every day a distinguished professor from my college walks in. What can I do for you?"

"You know me?"

"Well, I was pre-law, but I had to take some science classes to meet the distribution requirements, and I took an introductory physics course you gave. I was one of two hundred students in the lecture hall, so I don't expect you to remember me."

I tried to remember when I would have given such a class. "Introduction to Physics?"

"I don't remember what its name was. Everyone called it 'Quarks for Dorks.' It was for people like me, with no background in science and unlikely to do anything more with it. Instead, I ended up heading up the trust and estates department at Marx & McCormick." She paused, and took her sip from the travel mug on her desk. "So, what can I do for you?"

"I'm trying to find out about the Alison Gondelman Trust, particularly the house on Woodbine Avenue."

Ms. Chang took on a more serious expression. "Well, there's only so much I can tell you without violating attorney-client confidentiality. What is it you want to know?"

"I'm wondering if you have any idea of the whereabouts of Alison Gondelman." She looked at me oddly, and I thought I ought to explain my interest. Fortunately, I had come prepared. "You may know I hold the chair in physics named for her father, and I'm hoping she might get me access to some of his papers." If she bothered to check up on my story, she'd discover that there were indeed two boxes of his papers in the university archives that remained under seal.

"It's kind of funny," she began, pulling a folder from a side cabinet and placing it on her desk. "When we got your call, I looked at the file. Of course I wasn't here when the trust was set up back in the 1970s, but I became the trustee of record when Mr. Marx retired in 2011. I hadn't looked at it in quite a while, since we have staff to handle the mundane chores of making payments or contracting to have the property maintained. Frankly, I was hoping you were going to be able to tell us where she is. We've had no contact with her since long before I joined the firm in 2002. Other than our making monthly deposits to a passbook savings account to which we have no other access, there's really been no contact at all."

I was disappointed, of course, but I was used to that by now. After all these years, I was no longer surprised when I hit another dead end. However, something she said twitched at the edge of my consciousness. "You mentioned that you've hired someone to see that the property is maintained. Can't the people you've rented it to do that?"

It was the attorney's turn to look puzzled. "What people? That house has remained unoccupied since 1979. Our instructions were to maintain appearances, pay the real estate taxes and utilities, and see that it remain fit for occupancy. We have no authority to rent or sell it. In fact, the trust specifically bars us from doing so."

"I've been to the house and I saw a name on the mailbox. If they're not renters, then who are the Ceriers? Are they the caretakers?"

"Professor Price, I want to be helpful, but I really don't know what you're talking about. I don't know anyone by that name, and the house is unoccupied."

It took all my willpower not to bolt from the room like a madman. "Perhaps I was misinformed by one of the neighbors," I said, rising. "I'm sorry to have taken up your time."

"No problem at all, professor," she said, coming around to lead me out of the offices. She was probably just as relieved to see me going as I was to be getting out of there. "But if you should happen to hear from Alison Gondelman…"

"Yes?"

"Please have her get in touch with us."

I had no conscious memory of getting from the law offices to the Gondelman house. Sure enough, the name on the mailbox beside the door said, "Cerier." Indeed, it was done with those little metallic stick-ons that you have to buy a letter at a time. When I was last there, I thought it was just a piece of paper that had been taped to the mailbox. Something truly crazy was going on, and I was only about 80% certain that it wasn't me.

"Alison! Alison, are you in there? Open up!" I banged on the door and rang the bell, but there was no response. "Alison, it's Willy!"

"Hey, mister, nobody's home." I turned to look at a thirty-something woman with curly brown hair and two toddlers—clearly her own—whom she was barely managing to control. She was standing in the front yard of the house next door. "Tommy, let Timmy play with the ball. You had your turn."

"Have you seen the woman who lives here?"

"Timmy, stop kicking your brother. No, she's hardly ever around. When we moved in a couple of years ago, I was told that's one of the great mysteries of the neighborhood. You know how every place has one house where no one ever seems to be around, but you know people are coming and going? All right, both of you are getting a time out!"

The woman started taking her kids into her house. I shouted after her. "Wait, have you ever seen her? Do you know what she looks like?"

"Sorry, mister, I've got my hands full with these two." And she was gone.

In another minute, so was I, tearing back to campus to test my newest improvement to what was now Device 5.0. There was someone I needed to see. He had been avoiding me long enough. If I couldn't reach him in the past, I would have to go to the future.

T he new version was all set to be tested. It not only had the capacity to record and remember every place and time it went to, but I had manually entered the dates I had travelled to from the previous devices. I had kept records and, of course, I didn't need to bother with the 1977-1979 travels, which consisted of the bulk of the trips and which still remained closed to me. For this trip, I didn't have to search through the record. I simply went to the furthermost date I had, hoping that I would arrive at the same time. I was off by five minutes, and made a mental note to look into fixing that later.

It was 2187, and there was nothing to see but the two chairs surrounded by vague nothingness… and Cort, still dressed in his robe. He looked up in surprise. "Willy, what are you still doing here? You have to go."

It was only moments after I had left. "I did go, Cort. Look at me."

He stepped back, and looked me up and down. "You look terrible. Haven't you been keeping up with your treatments?"

"What treatments?"

"Your youth treatments… Oh, wait, that's much further down your timeline. Never mind. Forget I said anything."

"Cort, I know that to you, I just left, but for me, more than twenty years have gone by. I need something from you."

He frowned. "You know I can't tell you anything about the far future…"

"That's not what I'm asking for. I need you to listen to me carefully. I have reason to believe that you know—or can get to people who know—where Henry Gondelman is."

Cort looked at me with what I assumed was an expression of making an official pronouncement. "I can neither confirm nor deny that."

I gave him a rueful smile. "Thank you for confirming my suspicions, Cort."

He looked upset. "But I didn't say anything."

"You didn't have to," I replied. "If you knew nothing, it wouldn't have been a problem for you simply to say that."

"I told them I was no good at this," he pouted. "Willy, I wish I could help you, but I'm bound not to tell you anything."

"Then don't. Let me tell you something. I want you to deliver a message to Henry, or to someone who can see to it that he gets it. I want him to know that I have had it with him and his games and his rules and his formulas. I need to see him, and I need him to come immediately back to my time. And if he ignores me and doesn't clean up the mess he's made, then I won't be responsible for my actions."

Cort looked frightened, like a child seeing a parent lose his or her temper. "Don't do anything rash, Willy," he said anxiously, before asking, "Um, what *would* you do?"

I showed him the device. "This is version 5.0. I think I'm ready to stop tinkering and start exploring. Big time. If I'm able to remove his mother from her time line, would he still be born? Interesting question. Tell him I'm ready to find out."

"Willy, don't," said Cort, now seeming truly distressed. He took me by the shoulders, "I'll get a message to him. I can't say how, but I'll tell him you're desperate to see him."

"Thank you," I said, already feeling a bit calmer.

"Is that really Device 5.0?" He seemed genuinely curious.

"Why, yes. Coming to you was its shakedown cruise."

He gasped. "I don't know if I can take two historical encounters in a single day."

"What do you mean?"

"Willy, that's it. You've perfected the Time Travel Device. I can't believe I've met you at the start and the end of the process on the very same day."

Now I was puzzled. "Cort, we're more than a century beyond my time. Are you saying they haven't come up with any further improvements?"

"Not really. Oh, you can get it in various colors now, and I think there was a version that came out ten years ago that could also take your temperature and blood pressure, but those were more novelties than improvements."

I sensed he was going to go on in this vein, so I cut him short. "Thank you, Cort. I knew I could count on you."

"This was already the most memorable day of my life. It's all going to seem anticlimactic after this."

I patted him on the shoulder. "Cheer up. You'll be able to dine out on this story for years. Maybe even centuries."

I made ready to go, and he leaned in to embrace me. I'd become even less touchy-feely over the years, but I accepted his hug. What surprised me was when he leaned in close and whispered into my ear, "Hang in there, Willy. It's almost done."

He stepped back and gave me a wink. Before I could say anything further, he reached over and pressed the return button, another innovation for Device 5.0. As I was whisked back to my own time, I thought that if I ever get to write that definitive treatise on time travel, I'm going to dedicate it to Cort.

"It's about time you got here."

I had returned to my office, and barely had time to reorient myself. I wasn't alone. Seated at my desk was a woman roughly my age, a few grey streaks in her dark hair, and a not very happy expression on her face. It took me a moment to process this.

"How did you get in here?" I blurted out.

"Really? After all these years, not even a hello? A kiss on the cheek?"

"The door was locked," I stupidly continued.

"Willy, when was the last time the locks were changed for this office? I still had my key, and it still worked. It's probably how my father got in as well."

Finally the jumble of puzzle pieces settled into place. It was Alison. After all these years of searching and longing, here she was. She stood up. With tears in my eyes, I stepped forward to take her in my arms. Instead she slapped me.

"Alison!? What was that for?"

With a cold look on her face, she said, "You bastard. It took you almost twenty-five years to knock on my door? What took so long? Were you too busy?"

I was stunned. What had happened to her? And why was she blaming me for it? I had done everything in my power to find her. I leapt at every new opportunity almost the moment it came to my attention. I longed to pour my heart out to her. Instead, still feeling the impact on my cheek, I let a different part of my brain take over. "What took *me* so long? What about you? Where and when did you end up? And who's been living in your house?"

She turned away from me in disgust, swinging back around when she reached the windows at the back of the office. "Where was I? When I pressed that damned button, I found myself alone with my cat on the bench. You had disappeared. I had no idea what happened."

"Did it not work?"

"Oh, it worked all right. On my way back to house—on foot, carrying Spock—I picked up a newspaper. I was in 1997. My first thought was to call you, but then I realized that the 1997 you might not even have gotten the time machine yet. I didn't know what would happen if I contacted you before we met. And I was afraid to use the machine again. I considered myself lucky. I could have ended up in the Stone Age, for all I knew."

"So what did you do?"

"What *could* I do? I had to wait out the two years and hoped you returned on the same date in 1999. In the meantime, I had the house and

I had more money than I knew what to do with. The bank account my father had set up hadn't been touched in nearly twenty years. When I first went into the bank, there was some issue over IDs, but I had my birth certificate and a copy of the trust documents—my father really did save everything—and I found out that each time the deposits and interest hit the Federal insurance limit, the excess was rolled over into another account. I walked out of the bank with money in my purse and a bag full of savings account passbooks. Then I went home to wait."

"For two years?" I couldn't believe what I was hearing.

"I had enough to keep me occupied. The first thing I had to do was figure out what to do about any neighbors who still lived in the neighborhood and might have known me back in 1979. They might start wondering why I hadn't aged a day while they had aged eighteen years. Since anything addressed to Alison Gondelman was going to Dad's lawyers, I put another name on the mailbox. I might look like someone who used to live there long ago, but now I was Alice Cerier."

"Where the hell did 'Cerier' come from?"

She waved her hand in dismissal. "He was a friend of Dad's from his school days at MIT. He had been best man at my parents' wedding."

"Did it occur to you that when I showed up in 1999, desperately hoping you would be there, I saw the name 'Cerier' on the mailbox and assumed the house had been sold or rented?"

"So you were confused. Was your finger broken as well?"

I was beginning to wonder if she was suffering from dementia. She was making no sense. "My finger?"

She jabbed at the air. "You couldn't ring the bell and ask?"

"And ask what?" A few moments ago, my heart had been breaking with joy, and now I was furious. How dare she blame me. "I was 29 years old. As far as I knew, some stranger lived there. What was I to say? 'Hello, twenty years ago, the love of my life lived here. I was nine at the time. Do you know what became of her?' I would have been lucky not to be arrested."

"That was always your problem, Willy, playing it safe."

"Damn it, Alison! What was wrong with *your* finger? I've been easy enough to find on campus? Why didn't you call me? Why are you putting this all on me?"

"Because of my idiot father." We both turned to look at the speaker, a distinguished and vigorous looking white-haired woman who must have been at least eighty if she was a day. Her hair was pulled back in a longish pony tail, which served to accent her cheekbones. Her tailored black outfit was highlighted by the emerald green kerchief she wore around her neck. There was something familiar about her.

Before I could respond, Alison shouted at her, "Do you mind? This is a private conversation."

"And that's why there's every reason I have to stay. Don't either of you know who I am?" I was becoming annoyed that my office was turning into Grand Central Station, but we both took a good look at the intruder. I think we both realized who it was at the same time, but Alison couldn't bring herself to accept it.

"You're Alison, aren't you? From much further in the future."

She gave me the smile that I longed to get from the woman on the other side of the room, who was glaring at the older woman in shock. "You can't be me. You're *old*!" She blurted out, as much an accusation as an observation.

"I'm rubber, you're glue," the Older Alison began in singsong.

"Ladies. Er, Alisons. Let's stay calm," I turned to Older Alison, "Besides, you're not that old. What are you, 60? 65?"

She laughed. It was a laugh I had longed to hear again for nearly half my life. "Oh, Willy, you're such a charmer." She came over and patted the same cheek that Younger Alison had struck. "It's why I always loved you."

"Well, I…" I think I may have blushed.

"Sit, Willy. I need to have a conversation with myself."

I took the seat Alison had vacated, and watched as the woman I had been carrying a torch for all these years proceeded to start yelling at herself.

"You're going to stop this at once," she said, as if Younger Alison was her daughter.

"You're not the boss of me," she answered, somewhat petulantly I thought.

"Alison, I *am* you. And I've come here to prevent you from making a terrible mistake."

"You're about forty years too late for *that*," she said, glaring at me. Ouch.

"Alison," Older Alison shouted, "Shut up! You don't have the slightest clue what you're talking about."

Younger Alison was having none of this. "You mean I don't know how I've wasted my life, waiting for Professor Timemaster to find my front door."

I was hoping this wasn't going to come to blows. I didn't relish trying to break up a fight between the two of them. Older Alison then did something totally unexpected. She grabbed two of Younger Alison's fingers and bent them backwards. Younger Alison started to scream until the older woman said, "I'm not letting go until you shut up and listen." She kept applying pressure.

"Okay, okay, I'll listen!"

"Good," said Older Alison. "I had been hoping that physical force wouldn't be necessary." She released the fingers of her younger self. Turning to me, she said, "You're even for the slap now. Let's not ever refer to this momentary lapse again."

My head was spinning at this point. I was speechless. Meanwhile, Younger Alison was rubbing the fingers of her sore hand. "All right, you have my attention. What do you have to say? Get it over with."

She positioned herself between us and took a deep breath. "You two love each other, deeply and strongly." Younger Alison started to object, but was silenced with a glance. "I'm not telling you how to feel. I'm telling you how *I* feel after years and years of living with the love of my life. And much as I regret the time we were kept apart through no fault of our own, I have hated the fact that I was the one responsible for our being separate for another five years."

I liked the idea of our getting back together at last, but I was having trouble following this. "What's this about another five years?"

She turned to me. "Willy, I'm sorry, but I foolishly blamed you for this, and in another few minutes, I was going to walk out of your life, hoping never to see you again. Five years from now we meet again, both of us bitter and alone, and realize what a horrible mistake we made. We've been together ever since. I've learned there's nothing that I can do about the time you two have already been apart, but I can make sure that that ends here. This is something that *can* be changed."

"Oh, so I have to forgive him because my future self says so? Don't I have any say in the matter?"

The old woman sighed. "Of course you do. You can walk right out of here when I'm done and punish yourself because you think it will prove something. I'm here to tell you that *I* did just that, and it's one of the biggest regrets of my life."

Younger Alison seemed to consider this. "But I'm still angry at him. He made no effort to find me."

"That's not true…" I began.

"Willy, let me," Older Alison said with a smile. "He's spent more than twenty years looking for you. He tried to go back to just before the two of you left 1979, and found that the whole two and a half year period you were together was closed off to him. He constantly searched databases for any mention of us, hoping that there would be some clue. He checked alumni records. He was at the house today because he found out that it was supposed to be unoccupied."

Finally, I couldn't take it anymore. "And you were here all along. For God's sake, Alison, why didn't you just call me?"

"Because I told her not to."

The three of us turned to face the older man who had suddenly appeared in the room. "Dad!" the two Alisons shouted at once. It was, indeed, Henry Gondelman, looking no more than ten years older than when I had last seen him, all those years ago, and a few years younger than the older version of his daughter.

"You know, maybe I should just install a revolving door in here," I said to no one in particular.

Older Alison glared at her father. "Why don't you tell her why she couldn't call Willy?"

Henry looked at me and gave me a little wave. "You've been doing nice work."

"Dad!" yelled Younger Alison. "You specifically instructed me that the very structure of the space-time continuum was in danger of collapsing in upon itself if I didn't wait for him to contact me."

I look at her. "And you believed that bullshit?"

Older Alison put her arm on my shoulder. "Cut me some slack, Willy. I was young, lost, and alone in the future, and my father had always looked out for me." Then she spun on Henry. "But what the hell was *your* excuse? What possible reason could you have for feeding me that cock and bull story?"

"Yes, I want to hear this," chimed in Younger Alison.

Henry looked down at the floor for a moment, as if he was afraid to meet any of our eyes. "I know it was hard on both of you—er, all of you

—but it was necessary. I've been trying to unravel the mystery of where the Device originated ever since I was able to build my own. While mine was the first in the timeline, it was a copy of Willy's. And Willy never would have received it from himself if he hadn't finally perfected it… which I believe you've just done," he said at last, looking at me. "In fact, in just a few years, you'll be going back to 1997 to give your younger self Device 1.0. The theory is that you may have invented it yourself originally, but that may have been erased through revisions in the timeline when you gave it to your earlier self."

"What does this have to do with anything?" demanded Younger Alison.

"Well, once Willy had the Device, it would take a number of things to happen for him to perfect it. He had to come back to meet me. He had to get hold of my notebooks. He had to figure out how to apply my theoretical musings to the practical matter of traveling through time. We came to realize that the only way that would happen was if he was undistracted."

This was getting into serious mental overload territory again. "Who is 'we'?"

"I really can't say much. As you have no doubt figured out from your own travels, there are rules and enforcement authorities, the traffic cops of time travel, if you will. When I first encountered them and they realized who I was, they invited me to join them. That's why I've only been able to send occasional notes. I've been very busy."

I couldn't believe what I was hearing. Were we supposed to be sympathetic to his workload? "This is all fascinating, Henry, but you screwed up my life and, worse, you screwed up your daughter's life. Don't you think I could have perfected the Device *and* been happily married to the woman who had become my reason for being?"

Younger Alison seemed startled. "Really?"

"I've never stopped loving you," I said to her. I returned my focus to Henry. I was furious with him. "Well, what do you have to say for yourself, you pompous windbag? The great theoretician is suddenly at a loss for words? Why couldn't Alison and I be together?"

"I know you're upset, Willy, but I worked out the calculations every way I could, and then they were worked over in ways I'm still trying to grasp. You know how you couldn't save Lincoln? I couldn't bring the two of you together. Time just wouldn't permit it."

"But why? She was working on her philosophy treatise. How could that have possibly prevented me from getting my work done?"

"Well, it wasn't so much the marriage that was the problem as it was the distraction of fatherhood. See, you weren't going to be able to…"

I don't know what it was that I wasn't going to be able to do, because I was getting out of my seat to throttle him. My way was blocked by the two Alisons, who got to him first. "Dad," yelled the younger one, "He doesn't know."

"Oh," replied Henry, "You haven't told him about his son yet?"

At this, Older Alison gave him a smack on the back of the head. She turned to Younger Alison. "I know this is going to be hard for you to believe right now, but eventually you both forgive him." She smacked him again. "But not today. I think it's time for you to go. You're the perfect example of the scientist who doesn't have a clue about the impact of his work. It's long past time that you should read my book."

"My book? You mean I finally finish it?" Younger Alison seemed both startled and pleased by this news, but her older self simply held up a finger to cut off further discussion.

Turning back to Henry she repeated, "It's time for you to go. In fact, you should already be gone."

Henry puffed himself up. "I am still your father."

"And I'm your elder. Now get the hell out of here before I smack you a third time."

A chastened Gondelman headed to the door. "I'm truly sorry about all of this. But the hard part really is over. It all works out in the end, just like I promised."

Before any of us could answer, he pulled out his device. It was trimmed in blue. "I hope to see you both some time." He pressed a button and vanished.

I turned to the Alisons. "My son?"

The two women exchanged looks. "I think my work here is done," said Older Alison. "I need to get home, and you two have a lot of catching up to do. I hope you'll do the right thing." She embraced her younger self.

"Thank you," said Younger Alison. "We probably won't be meeting again…"

The older woman laughed. "Given enough Time, anything is possible." Then she turned to me. "And it was a pleasure to see you again." I prepared myself for a hug, but she moved right in and planted a big kiss right on my lips.

"I…"

"Don't spoil the moment, Willy. I can't wait to get home and tell you that I was fooling around with a younger man today." She pulled out her own device which, I noted, was color coordinated with her kerchief. "You kids have fun." With that, she slipped away into time.

Alison and I were now alone. There was an awkward silence. "You know, you were two years younger than me," I began. "Since you arrived in 1997 you gained two years before we were back in sync. Now we're the same age."

"Don't spoil the moment, Willy," she said, as time stood still and she slipped into my arms.

GOOD NIGHT

"Your son? Is that what this has been all about?" Miller had gotten up, and was looking down at the professor still seated on the bench. "A whole day telling me this epic saga, just so you could claim to be my missing father?"

"It's not a claim, Max. Ask your mother. We tried to figure out the best way to break the news to you, and this seemed to be the most effective. If I had just blurted it out when we first met, you wouldn't have believed me."

The reporter had an unreadable expression on his face. "I'm not sure I believe you now."

"I assume you saw where this was going when I told you how your mother had assumed the name Cerier."

"I don't know what you're talking about," said the younger man. "My last name is Miller."

Price sadly shook his head. "No, it's not, Max. That's your middle name."

After a moment of tense silence, the reporter slumped his shoulders, admitting defeat. "I was tired of explaining to people that it was pronounced with a hard C and not a soft one. You know how, when you're a kid, anything that makes you different leads to teasing? When I started writing for the college paper, I realized I could choose my own byline, and I became Max Miller," he sighed. "So assuming I believe your story, do I have to change it to Gondelman or to Price?"

The professor stood up. "Max, you don't have to do anything you don't want to do. We were both cheated. You grew up without a father, and I missed raising my son. You're an adult now. We can't make up for the time we lost. All I can do is hope that we've started to build a relationship."

The reporter mulled that over for a bit. Finally he asked, "And have you forgiven Henry?"

"Your mean your grandfather? Not yet. But I suppose we will eventually."

They started to walk across the quad. There was no one in sight as they headed in the direction of the parking lot. Even the library had closed for the night, and the buildings were mostly dark. "So, Willy, what do you want from me? Do you expect me to write up your story without any proof?"

"What you write or don't write is your choice, Max. You have free will. There may be rules in place, but how you respond to circumstances is entirely up to you. I'm kind of hoping that you'll join the family business."

They had reached the front of the Physics Building, and Miller stopped dead in his tracks. "The family business? What are you talking about? I'm not a scientist. I'm just another ink-stained scribbler."

Price smiled. "Which is exactly what we need. Your grandfather is the theoretician. I'm the practical scientist figuring out the applications. Your mother is building a grand philosophic discourse. We need to add someone like you to the mix."

"To do what? Write your biography?"

"No," replied the professor. "To do the user's manual."

"Excuse me?"

"Look at all the problems I had. If the device is going to go into wider use, it needs a set of instructions that clearly states what can and cannot be done, how to prepare for one's travels, what to do if you get separated from your party, and so on. You're used to gathering information and then explaining it to the public so that the average person can make sense of it. You're precisely what we need."

"And I'm just supposed to quit my job to do this?"

Price shook his head. "Of course not. I'm still teaching here, aren't I? It's your mother's side of the family that lives in the world of ideas and is fortunate enough to have sufficient income to be able to afford it. You're my son as well. We're practical men. You can keep your outside work as long as you want to, and as long as it's satisfying. We just want to put your skills to use as well. And that's why I want to give you this."

Price reached into his briefcase and pulled out what looked like a small electronic device. It was, in fact, the Device. Miller took it. "This is it? This will let me flit through space and time?"

"Well, within limits. That's what you need to discover and explain to everyone else."

Miller stared at it. "It doesn't look very special."

Price gave a rueful smile. "They don't add color trim for another fifty years, or so I'm told."

"You know, I still haven't said whether I believe any of this."

The professor took the reporter's arm. "That's why I'm entrusting you with this. I want you to try it out on your own terms, to see for yourself," he said. He paused, and then added, "And I hope, Max, that I can get something from you in return."

Miller looked at the older man. "What?"

"Your story. You know all about me now and, except for what your mother has told me, I know very little about you. I would love to have a day when I'm your audience, and you tell me all about your loves and hopes and dreams and disappointments. You're my son, and we have a lifetime of catching up to do. I want to know who *you* are."

If Miller had any trace of cynical doubt left in him, that last speech dissolved it. He embraced the professor. "Daddy," he said simply.

When they stepped back, Price straightened his jacket and said, "Now, now, there's no need for that. I told you to call me Willy."

The reporter wiped his eyes. "Is it all right if I call you Dad?"

"You can call me anything you want," replied Price. "Just don't call me late to supper."

Miller winced. "Really? Really? The father of time travel likes stupid old jokes?"

Price shrugged his shoulders. "What can I say? After all those years apart from your mother, I look for any opportunity to have a bit of fun and enjoy myself. I have a bit of catching up to do myself."

The younger man's smile turned into a yawn. "And I think that what I need to do now is catch up on my beauty rest. I'm going to go home and sleep and, sometime tomorrow afternoon when I wake up, figure out what I'm going to do next."

"If I might make a suggestion…?"

"After all this, *now* you need my permission to speak?"

Price chuckled. "I supposed I have run on a bit," he said. "You're right. I think you do want to get a full night's rest before beginning any extensive experimentation with the Device. However, I think you'll sleep a lot easier if you give it a quick test now, just so you'll know that it really works and you didn't imagine everything that happened today."

Miller looked puzzled? "A test? To where... or should I say, 'To when?'"

"There's no reason you couldn't do this tomorrow, or even next year, for that matter, but I think you'll find it more dramatically satisfying if you do it right now."

Price took the Device back from Miller and began setting the coordinates. The reporter looked puzzled. "Dramatically satisfying? Where are you sending me?"

"To the other side of the quad at about 3 o'clock this afternoon. I believe you have a text message that you'd like to send."

It took a moment for what Price was saying to register, and then Miller got it. "Oh, yes. Oh my, yes. I definitely need to send that text message right away."

Price pointed to the controls. "You press this button to go and this one to return. I think you'll quickly figure out how it works. I made it so that it's user friendly. That's why creating a user's manual is so important, but you'll have plenty of time to get into that. For now, go take it out for a spin."

Miller took the Device back. "Thanks... Dad."

Price started to choke up. "You're welcome... son. Now get out of here before we both start crying like two-year-olds. And when you get back, go home and get some rest."

"When will I see you again?"

Price burst into a big smile. "Whenever you want, Max. Whenever you want."

Max smiled back, pressed the button, and vanished.

Now alone, Price headed up to his office. The building was unlocked at night, even if the offices were all shuttered and dark. The sole exception to this was his own office. He opened the door and saw he was not alone.

"It's about time you got here."

"You know, I really have to get that lock changed."

He and Alison embraced for a good long moment. Finally she asked, "He knows? You told him?"

"I told him everything."

"And he believed you?"

"Not for most of the day, but I think when he tried the Device for himself, any remaining doubts vanished." Price gave her a big smile. "I can't believe I finally have you back, and I got a son in the bargain as well."

A sad look flitted across her face. "I'm sorry that you missed his growing up. I've got tons of pictures to show you. You could have played catch with him."

"You mean I might have scarred him for life when he discovered what a klutz his father is."

Alison took his hand. "All right, then, you might have bought him his first chemistry set."

"Chemistry!? Please, dear, I'm a physicist."

"You're off duty now, Willy. Shouldn't we be getting home?"

They headed to the door, and Willy clicked off the lights. They walked hand in hand all the way to the parking lot. They had so much catching up to do, but they were no longer in any hurry.

After all, they had all the Time in the world.

ACKNOWLEDGMENTS

In some ways this book completes a trilogy of science fiction books, although they are unrelated and you don't need to have read all of them... although you should. *Jar Jar Binks Must Die* and *Shh! It's a Secret*, as well as *Time on My Hands*, came to fruition during a very tough period of my life. This book was written as I began to emerge on the other side.

So I need to begin by thanking the many people who helped me weather the storm. This is not a complete list by any means, and if I overlooked you I apologize. My gratitude is no less sincere. Nonetheless I'm going to try: Betty Przewuzman Smithline, Dr. Davin Wolok, Michael Devney, Robert Devney, Stephen Karpf, Esq., Tom Easton, Michael and Nomi Burstein, Jennifer Pelland, Bonnie-Ann Lynch Black, John Glindeman, Rabbi Eliana Jacobowitz, Seth Weiss, Charles Munitz, David Leibowitz, Shannon McCarthy, LICSW, Maura Moran, Steve Baturin, David Kaplan, Dan Miller, Dr. Gary and Minda Login, Walter and Lisa Hunt, Mark and Evelyn Leeper, Nat Segaloff, Chris Garcia, Dan Schweiger, Rabbi Charles Simon, Rabbi Leonard Gordon, Elliot Feldman, Kilian Melloy, Monica Castillo, Tim Estiloz, and—always—Sido Surkis.

Next I have to say something about the names in the book. Yes, Dr. Surkis clearly is named for my dear friend, but several other names are there because over the last few years I've lost a number of much older friends at Congregation Mishkan Tefila, one of my two synagogues. Adapting an old Jewish tradition, I have named my characters for them, at least in part, but it should be clear that I borrowed only the names, and that the real people were nothing at all like the characters depicted here. Nonetheless, I want to recall Mel Miller, Morty Gondelman, Bill "Willy" Ehrlich, and Mel Cerier. They are missed and, as we say in Hebrew, "*zichro livracha*" (may each of their memories be a blessing).

I also have to provide a shout-out to my young colleague, film critic Charlie Nash. In spite of making me feel like Methuselah when he noted that he read one of my reviews "as a child," he also provided some unplanned inspiration for one of the novel's plot twists. It was and is appreciated. A special thank you must also go to Bill Ricker, and the other perpetrators and hosts of "Maltcon," a floating party at several science fiction conventions where I was taught how to drink and appreciate single malt scotch. I'm not quite a convert, but I was and am an apt pupil, and I raise a dram to toast those who helped provide the background for Professor Price's drinking preferences.

My editor and publisher, Ian Randal Strock, is also a friend—and how many writers can say that? This is my third book with him, and I can say two important things about our working relationship: his editorial comments were helpful, particularly in a story bouncing around in time, and his checks always clear.

My long time agent Alison Picard has now seen me through six books. May there be many more.

Finally, my daughter, Amanda wasn't even born when I worked on my first book but she has been mentioned in every book I have done since then. This one will be no exception. She remains the light of my life, and as I enjoy telling people, as a father I'm expected to love my daughter. I also *like* her. I hope she likes this book.

—Daniel M. Kimmel
October 2016

CPSIA information can be obtained
at www.ICGtesting.com
Printed in the USA
LVOW08s0740060417

529842LV00001B/125/P